I0555839

Dead Signals//
Lost Transmissions

A Neon Sunrise Anthology

ISBN: 978-1-7357360-7-5

Original cover art created by Tim Shubert

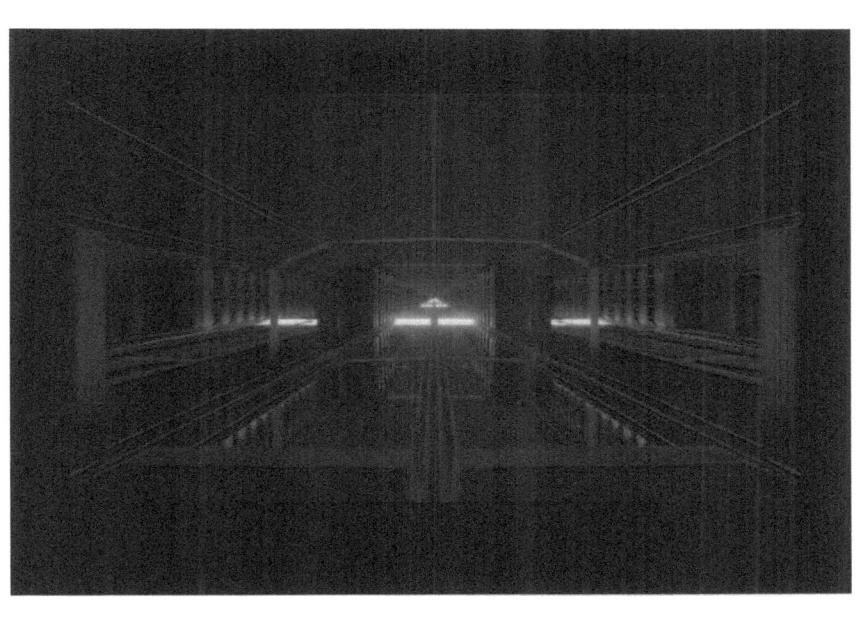

Introduction

Do you remember the first time you were captivated by a story in the realm of science fiction? The sense of wonder it brought you? For me, two movies immediately pop into my head – Star Wars and E.T. I was a small child but I remember them both vividly. Star Wars brought adventure and battles in far off outer space, and E.T. was the first movie I ever saw at the movie theater. I loved E.T. trying to get home and was terrified of the people in hazmat suits! Both of those films started me on a journey into the pictures and pages of science fiction and began a lifelong love affair with the genre.

Fast forward 40 years and through numerous books by the likes of Phillip K. Dick, Isaac Asimov, Robert Heinlein, Edgar Rice Burroughs, William Gibson, Ursula K. LeGuin, Frank Herbert, Orson Scott Card, and many more and you'll find that love affair has only deepened. I truly <u>love</u> Scifi as a genre in all mediums. The potential for amazing stories is boundless no matter what genre you choose to settle into, but I find myself consistently drawn back to the well of stars and remote galaxies – the alternate universes and distant histories – in the imaginative corners of Scifi.

When it came time to decide on the next projects for Neon Sunrise, I knew without question that we had to put together a Scifi genre anthology. *Dead Signals//Lost Transmissions* is something special to me, and I'm happy that it's finally in your hands (or on your screen). Within its pages run the gamut of themes and ideas that will be familiar and refreshing, from time travel and cybernetics to vast space and existential terror. If you love this genre as much as I do then there's so much in this book for you to love.

10 authors from the US and UK answered the call for submissions and poured their digital souls into the poetry and stories now at your fingertips. It is our hope that you find the joy and excitement in these pages that we've all found in writing them. We hope it kindles a love for new authors and sparks your desire to seek out more.

There is so much to see out there. The universe is vast and possibly a touch overwhelming, but awe inspiring and exciting too. We believe that Scifi opens a door to those possibilities and this is our offering to you. Step through the portal with us and let's see where it goes!

See you where the sidewalk ends,
David Greshel
June 2022

Acknowledgements

There are so many things that go into putting a book together. Neon Sunrise may be a one-person operation on paper, but none of this would be possible without the support of so many different people.

Thank you to friends and family for the encouragement and shared excitement to see this project come to life.

Thank you to everyone that supported the Kickstarter campaign and shared in the marketing and promotion.

Thank you Davy, Heidi, Stephanie, Heather, Steve, Frank, Peter, Stephen, and Leanne. For wanting to be a part of this project and for providing your amazing talent. This book doesn't exist without you, and I'm grateful that you've trusted me to bring your work to the world.

Thank you to Tim Shubert for providing the original art used for the cover. I'm continually impressed by your dedication to your art and I'm thankful for the years of friendship we've shared.

Additional Art Credits

Pg. 3 – Hannes Werder
Pg. 9 – Sergei Tomakov
Pg. 61 – Saumya Shukla
Pg. 87 – Steve Zmijewski
Pg. 98 – Douglas-Dragonboy7557
Pg. 141 – Tim Shubert

A special acknowledgement and an extra-sized thank you to all of the following people who helped bring this project to life on Kickstarter. Your sense of community and support is incredibly valuable and we could not have done this without you!

Travis Gibb
JonathanHedrickComics.com
Peter J. King
Davy Lee
Stephanie Guasp
You Rock Heidi!
Star Kaat
Danielle Montgomery
Joel Gonzalez
Leanne Kathleen Ingino
Nicole Widrig
Deb Walsh
Jennifer Knapp
Brian W
SC
TC
Christina Cardenas
Jonathan Mundell
Steve Zmijewski
S. R. Malone
Pete Riesett
Matt Kund
Rachel Mintz
Liz Lugo
Cliff Smithson
Bret Eayrs
Don Nguyen
Mary Berger
Rick Shea
Roselili Vargas
Kingdom of Comics
Finish Line Comics
Andew Abarca
Taurus Comics
Tom Sokolowski
Nancy Parker
Nicholas Stephenson
Zoe Kaplan
Joshua Dobbs
Chris Ballinger
Eron Wyngarde
Scott Schiffmacher

Thea Flurry
Joanne Williams
Rachel Carroll
Frontline Comics
Rebecca King

Davy Lee

The Class

Said Mr. H. Irving Hancock, "Every person must at one time learn to write letters!" His great mustache quivered and seemed to wave at us an invitation. Us being the class of girls at St. Gertrude's. Mr. H. Irving Hancock, the sub, took over at one point until he vanished, and left a grey bloomage on our lives and verbiage in his wake.

We, who were in the class, were, and are still, confused and affected by him. Nowadays, we're old but our paranoia ridden reminiscence always gets us back to squabbling as if again we are in those dusty halls and sitting behind the wooden desks.

We had a clue, even then, and still more today, that he was the confused time traveler that came to us one year for a brief time to teach us instead of Mrs. Peck, who was home pregnant and to burst any day. We don't share this story. No one is to know — there's no use anyhow as no one would believe us — and as far as we can tell it was only us that ever knew him.

"The first point to be observed in your letters is that you write in a clear, legible hand, a hand that anybody can read." A phrase from one of his first lessons. Then he wrote his name, which probably would have been very legible on a chalkboard. But the chalk left some faint blue streaks and scuff marks on the whiteboard. Mr. H. Irving Hancock seemed not to notice and turned to us for praise.

We imagine now what his eyes must have seen, lost in a sea of blank gazes mocking his out-of-time situation. He pulled hard on the curled ends of his mustache. We all sniggered and he blushed.

Billie thought he must be from the early nineteen-hundreds and basically, we all agreed. Some still think he was crazy — like Erin who said he was crazy and somebody should do something. Erin thinks we're the crazy ones now. When we thought this made some sense — to at least make aware of the situation to the outer world that time travel was possible — we told the principal and were accused of torturing poor Mrs. Peck. We reminded the principal there was a sub and to this he held tight to his repetitive words of shooing, "Nonsense, girls. Nonsense."

Our rap sheet betrayed us, and so we told our parents who said not to worry. That every sub seems like they're from another time. And our parents clinked their glasses and shared those woozy iridescent eyes that made us sick with thought of them together but also sick with desire and worry that someday we might mimic that kaleidoscope vision for others, even each other, that way someday. And of course, we did.

Said Mr. H. Hancock, "Ever has knowledge been so imperatively needed as it is to-day. The twentieth century opens with practically every approach to success barred to him who is not equipped with accurate information of the most varied kind."

Billie, who had had her fill of the charade, looked over her iphone with the look that said plainly *told you so*, but Erin was then still confused because the twentieth century had to be now and when we told her (showed her on Wikipedia) clearly we were in the twenty-first century she nearly tore out her braids saying, "We couldn't be in the twenty-first century when it was the year TWENTY-twenty and not twenty-ONE twenty." Words at that time, for some, were hard.

"The quadrille is the most universal, as it is certainly the most sociable of all fashionable dances." Mr. H. Irving Hancock clicked his heels and spun with an unexpected grace. The sight of him, and how Molly could tug on the cuffs of his grey tweed jacket (we had thought maybe our hands would pass straight through), could not resist but to dance too.

From then on, our math lessons were heralded with the "latest" dances. We picked our feet off the ground and though we danced how we knew, Mr. H. Irving Hancock, with his great mustache in swing and innocent loving smile briefly sparkling from beneath, bounced along encouragingly to the music Billie played from her iphone. Surprised, Mr. H. Irving Hancock, marveled at, "A little eraser that plays music. What an age!"

It was Sarah's idea to put to bed the issue once and for all.

We began to follow him home which was quickly abandoned on account we were expected home after school and the fact that afterwhile a heavy mist would roll in and we would lose him beneath the street lights.

We then simply snooped in his belongings for any hard clues, which was accepted. But not without most saying it was highly unprofessional if not indecent and not at all lady-like.

Said Jenny, "She should remember that, however welcome she may be, a lady is not always wanted."

Tara smacked Jenny and Jenny smacked her own, already reddening cheek. Although Casandra looked daggers at Tara and said underneath her breath which we could all hear, "Definitely not a lady." Mr. H. Irving Hancock's lessons divided us both mind and unit. All but when we danced or learned Jiu Jitsu, real fights would ensue but there isn't any need to rehash the ugly parts of the past.

So it was after the fire-alarm, which most first concluded was our scheme hatching as planned, turned into a real grease fire. Erin liked to smoke and was almost caught but threw it in the garbage next to the grease trap.

The cafeteria, in moments, was left with a smoldering hole where we would have lined and awaited our meals just an hour from when we yanked down the lever on the alarm. Gapped mouth from the soccer field, we watched the black smoke writhe into the grey sky shrouded in thick low clouds that seemed to suck up the smog and take it elsewhere like a great locomotive in the sky.

We blamed Erin for her bad habit and worse timing as all hopes to snoop through Mr. H. Irving Hancock's bag were dashed.

"You nasty thing you ruined it," said we.

But as soon as we were close to berating Erin to tears, Mr. H. Irving Hancock stepped through us with embers smoldering from the finely curled points on his mustache and shrunk us all in his wild eyes we hadn't seen before on a gentleman.

"Mr. H. Irving Hancock!" We said after him. "What's wrong?"

He replied, not affording us a glance but continued to flee, and in a voice nearly lost in the approaching song of fire engines, "The game of dominoes is frequently looked upon as a trivial amusement, but those who are well acquainted with it agree that it affords room for much curious calculation."

Having learnt from him, the blood boiled to our eyes and we called, marching after him in unison with accusing fingers raised, "In talking with ladies of ordinary education, avoid political, scientific, or commercial topics and choose only such subjects as are likely to be of interest to them."

We could care less about dominoes. We wanted answers for his visit. Our voices were raised and would not be drowned out.

He turned around on the soccer field. Twisted the burnt from the ends of his mustache and removed his bromley leather hat. The working stiff lid was removed, exposing a bald splotchy whiteness red with anger.

"I...I..."

We waited breathlessly for his words. But for the first and last time, he was speechless.

He stuffed his hands in his pockets forgetting he held his hat in one and dropped it. So lost within himself he didn't notice the hat slipped from his grip. Before we remembered to chase after him, he was gone and too was the hat. Caught in the wind and whirl of low black smoke that swirled and clouded our vision. The last we saw of him was his hat, nearly making it into the goal. A miss by inches.

When Mrs. Peck returned with the usual subjects we knew we missed the things we didn't know about the world, or at least what people in the world had thought about it and us. Even if it was the world of the TWENTIETH century, Erin.

Math and science were indeed even less interesting. Stephanie, the whiz kid, was too distracted to ace her algebra exams. After one such exam, Bethany raised her hand. Mrs. Peck said, with barely a glance in her direction, "You may go to the restroom."

Bethany lowered her quivering hand and stared into the computer screen and began to weep. We all began to weep. First Bethany. Then Stephanie, for what we thought was at least a little bit about her poor exam. Billie balled in her ugly way. And Jennifer, who had really been a silent partner in this adventure, let slip down her quiet mouth a tear.

Mrs. Peck made all the attempts in the world to calm us, but we would not be quelled. Cooed or otherwise. We wanted Mr. H. Irving Hancock. We wanted his ideas. We wanted to argue. All of his ideas on the world—math was more fun because we danced before. A dumb, silly dance we wouldn't be caught dead doing but we wanted to dance before algebra.

"Nonsense," said Mrs. Peck.

And then we knew that Mr. H. Irving Hancock was truly dead, and with it our escape that was childhood. We had grown up. He had grown us up by leaving. By existing as the last true magick that was all ours that no one knew about, and it was gone forever and the real world, our world, was the only world staring back at us through the wide windows and from far beyond the soccer field.

Some time later, in the Worrington Graveyard, we gathered to mourn. The graves were not alphabetical like Erin suggested they might be, but before midnight, and before the search parties were sent, we found a grave of a Hancock, or a Moorecock, or Hanfeld, but in any case the grave was too weathered and too disfigured to tell. Plus, many more than we would care to admit were past our bedtime.

So it was the grave that would do, for it was old and certainly from the turn of the previous century. At the right angle, tightening of the vision, and when the moonlight ducked from cover it looked like to read, *Mr. H. Irving Hancock, 1879 - 1935, A Man Like This Has Lived But Only Once.*

Said the class, "Sooner or later in our lives the sad time
comes, for who breathless must suffer, and who thinks must mourn,
and we have perforce to turn our minds to the inevitable and share
the common lot of man."

Billie laid the reef she wove from dandelions on the grave.
We bowed. We prayed. We sang "Yankee Doodle" under our breath
because we did not want to wake the ghosts that surely didn't like a
class of little girls out late at night. Which was all good and well as
we needed to save our energy to dance at the end.

We practiced Jiu-Jitsu in our mourning dress we found in
the theater costume room at school. Silk crapes, Henrietta, Albert
crape, Melrose, rainproof crape, silk, Cyprus crape. Janus Cord,
Victoria cord, Balmoral cloth, Cashmere francais, Kashgar Cashmere
and for those that ran warm wore drap dete. And if it wasn't actually
any of that, we pretended.

Said the class, "The principles of the Jiu-Jitsu system were kept secret, being passed down under oath from father to son. It was forbidden to show any of the tricks to any one not a member of the *Samurai*. In time, after months of practice, you will be able to throw an opponent, no matter how much stronger he is than yourself." We all felt like Samurai that night. Warriors who would take their own life in dishonour to their master. And together we committed seppuku, tugging red ribbons from beneath our shirts.

And finally, we danced until one by one we fell over graves, on tufts of grass, or in the folds of each other's sleeves and torn jeans, dreamily drafting a letter to our dear Mr. H. Irving Hancock:

Dear Mr. H. Irving Hancock,
We never once wrote a letter until now.

Sincerely,
The Class

Davy Lee is an MFA graduate in Creative Writing from the University of Central Florida and a BFA graduate in Creative Writing from Truman State University. His fiction work has been published in the 2016 Scythe Prize, the 2017 Scythe Prize, Windfall, The Gateway Review, and upcoming in Neon Sunrise Publishing. His non-fiction work won the Annie Dillard Award from St. Charles Community College. His first comic writing publication is upcoming in 2022 with Orange Cone Productions. On Thursday nights he teaches Creative Writing at a mall, but most days he works as a full time Reading teacher at a middle school.

Stephanie Guasp

Blank Slate

My voice is not butter
My voice is a spoon in the disposal
It's rough, and it demands action

My hips are not coke bottles
Not fragile, nor bending to please your eye
My hips are rocket ships
Powerfully, they propel me to new lands

My tongue is not silk, my lips are not petals
Not for stroking egos, nor whispering sweet nothings
My mouth is a weapon
Whether for peace or peril
I wield it with caution

My mind is not your canvas
No blank slate for keeping your favorite colors
My mind is a river
Winding neurons forge paths
Through the greyest of matter

My brain, a danger
A live wire, racing
A sure fire
Blazing

 Stephanie has been reading and writing poetry as far back as she can remember. From Shel Silverstein to Kahlil Gibran and everyone between, her thirst for beautiful language is insatiable. When she's not writing poetry, Stephanie enjoys penning lyrics and making music. She's also an avid gamer and doting dog mom to her 10-year-old lab mix, Bodhi. She's passionate about travel and can't wait to get back to Europe when the time is right. You can follow her for writing and photography on Instagram: @sguasp or check out her music on YouTube, channel name sguasp27.

Frank Martin

Lullaby

I'm so lucky. At least, that's what other parents tell me.

I give Lilly her bottle, she burps right away, and is asleep in the crib three minutes later. Once her favorite pink blanket is on her I can count on a solid two hours of alone time. That's the main reason why I let my wife go grocery shopping while I volunteer to stay home with the baby. Lord knows I wouldn't be able to handle the little rugrat if she just screamed her head off all day long.

Other parents also tell me that girls are easier than boys. Not that I have the experience to compare. But my wife and I were hoping for a girl from the moment she discovered she was pregnant. Besides the day she was born, finding out Lilly would be...well...Lilly was the best day of my life. Most guys pray for boys. But I wanted a princess to spoil. Not that we would love a boy any less. We would just have to try again on the next go around.

Even knowing how good Lilly is, though, I still want to keep an eye on her. Always. So before leaving her room I make sure the camera for the baby monitor is set up just right. It hasn't moved from its spot on top of the changing table across the room, but I double-check its angle anyway. From this far away I can see the whole room, crib included, which will come in handy when she starts standing in a couple months. But for now, this position is good enough so that I can spot her moving between the bars.

After leaving the nursery I head into our master bedroom and unplug the monitor from its charging station on the nightstand. The camera looked situated when I left the room, but I immediately turn the screen on just to be sure. Good. It's perfect.

With the monitor in hand, I carefully traverse back through the hallway and down our old staircase. When Lilly was first born it felt awkward tiptoeing around the house, but now I do it without a second thought. As girly as it might sound, I almost feel like a ballerina gently placing my feet down on the hardwood floors without a creek. Then again, I've learned that a lot of things a father has to do for his baby aren't the most masculine of activities. I've also learned to embrace them.

After clearing the stairwell, I jump down to the first floor's carpeting and that's when I know I'm safe. The soft floor doesn't make a sound as I head down the hall and into the den. My own personal man-cave of sports, video games, and everything in between. The missus says she's going to turn this into a playroom when it's time for us to make baby number two. But we've got years before that's happening (at least, I hope). For now, this twelve by twelve room is the only sanctuary I have in the house from the burp clothes and pacifiers.

I plop down on the sofa and pull back on the lever, shooting my feet up and my head back like a king on his reclining throne. The remote is peacefully waiting on the seat next to me and I snatch it up, swapping out the device by putting the baby monitor in its place. The screen is perfectly angled in the cushions so that I can see it just right from my side of the sofa. And I give it one good, concentrated stare to make sure all is right in the baby's room before clicking on the fifty-inch monster of an HDTV mounted on the wall in front of me.

The screen instantly beams a bright broadcast of college basketball into the room. My neck then drops back into the headrest, where my body plans on staying until the demands of fatherhood permit otherwise. Unfortunately, that moment comes sooner than I hoped when a sound from the monitor draws my attention.

Only the noise isn't the normal baby blabber I'm used to hearing. The small device lets out a short beep, and I turn my head to find that the screen has become all white with an error message reading "OUT OF RANGE."

How can this be? I've had this thing out in the yard and it's worked just fine. Why would it say out of range all of a sudden?

For a second I find myself struggling to breathe and frozen in my seat. I know it's probably nothing. Just a glitch or some kind of disruption in the signal. But not being able to see or hear my baby girl fills me with the crushing dread of an overly concerned parent.

I pick up the monitor and start randomly pushing buttons in the hope that something will bring it back to life. But nothing works. Should I run up there? Yeah, I should probably run up there.

I kick my legs back into the sofa, propelling myself forward out of the seat when the monitor's black and white picture suddenly reappears. An involuntary sigh of relief exits my lungs as I scan the screen to make sure everything's the same. I know it's just my paranoia. The monitor was down for only few seconds. What could possibly happen in that amount of time? But I check anyway and see the baby's outline lying peacefully through the bars of the crib. Good. Everything's as it should be.

My shoulders relax from the building tension, and I keep my eyes on the screen as I sit back down. I couldn't imagine what I would be feeling if the picture came back and Lilly was gone. As unlikely as that would be, I guess that's the ultimate nightmare for any parent: your child gone in an instant and there was nothing you could do about it.

Saying that my wife would kill me would be an understatement. Even after a couple months, she still worries every time I'm alone with the baby. And to be fair, I still give her reason to. Hell, I call looking after Lilly "babysitting," which my wife's all too happy to point out that it's not babysitting if you're watching your own child.

Not that it feels like babysitting. Lilly's just so simple. A bottle, burp, and diaper change later and I'm downstairs watching the basketball game with the monitor by my side.

Only a few seconds go by, though, before another sound grabs attention. But again, it's not Lilly or even the monitor beeping this time. It's voices. Whispers almost. And two of them.

Everything seems fine. I figure maybe its residual audio from the TV or something. That is until I see two dark figures pass in front of the camera.

Unlike before, when the blank screen only held the possibility of an unknown terror, my body recognizes the situation as an immediate threat and pours adrenaline into my muscles. Instinct immediately takes over, popping me of the seat and shooting me towards the stairs in a full on sprint. I stomp my way up every third step in a frantic scramble, catching a brief glimpse of the two robed figures still on the monitor. They're now leaning over the crib! I gotta get there!

At the top of the stairs I turn the corner of the hall and nearly dive head first through Lilly's doorway. My arms are up, my fists are clenched (with the monitor in my right hand) and I'm ready for action. But there's no one to be found. The room is empty. How can that be?

My eyes dart back over to the screen and the strange people in robes are still staring into the crib at my baby. My baby! But how?

Maybe the signals got crossed? I've heard stories about houses picking up on each other's baby monitors. Is that what I'm seeing? My freaky neighbors doing some bizarre ritual in robes?

No. I'm definitely looking at Lilly's room on the screen. Her crib, the curtains and pictures are all there. What am I even thinking? It's the same damn view I've been staring at for months!

And the strangest thing of all: I'm nowhere to be seen. I'm standing dead center in the middle of the room and should be on the monitor. The camera is right in front of me. The light is on. It's transmitting. Then why can't I see myself? Why aren't I on the screen? But strangers are. And now they're...they're reaching into the crib! My God! They're going to take Lilly!

My brain surges into a panic, but I don't know what to do. How could I? I don't even know what's going on.

My eyes start wildly scanning the room for something, anything that could give me a clue. But there's nothing out of the ordinary. The room is immaculate. Clean and perfect without the slightest hint that anything was wrong.

I dart back into the hall, desperately searching for a sign. Yet all I can hear is the basketball announcer's faint voice from the television still on downstairs.

Confusion clouds every one of my senses as I mope back into the nursery while staring at the screen. So much so that I didn't even realize had muddled my mind is. What am I worried about? The baby is right in front of me, peacefully sleeping in the crib. There's no one else in the room. How could they take her?

But even knowing all that, I still, once again, find myself holding my breath, hoping, praying that this is some mistake. That these people on the monitor are not about to grab my baby girl.

The robed couple continues to reach inside and spends a few seconds playing with whatever child's inside. They then lean out of the crib, turn to face the camera and my heart instantly drops into the pit of my stomach. Lilly is in their arms. My beautiful baby girl is laughing and smiling without a care in the world while two strangers are...wait. I can finally see their faces. Now, after finally turning around, I can see beneath the dark hoods of their robes and I can't believe my eyes. It's me and my wife, smiling just like the day Lilly was born.

I'm speechless. Dumbfounded. Completely and utterly baffled. My mind is racing through a crazy storm of disbelief. What in the hell is going on? How is this happening? And through it all, Lilly looks so happy, still wrapped in her favorite pink blanket.

The blanket!

In my crazy hysteria I didn't even notice the lack of pink in her crib. I take a step towards it and peer over the edge to see there's still a baby sleeping calmly inside. But its blanket isn't pink. It's black. Similar in color to the strange robes of my doppelganger.

And furthermore, the baby's face is familiar...but different. It looks like Lilly. Same nose and ears. But its features are more defined and heavy. No. It's definitely not Lilly. Because the baby in front of me is a boy.

Frank Martin is a comic writer and author that is not as crazy as his work makes him out to be...seriously.

Since his writing career began he's had multiple short stories published in horror anthologies by numerous indie publications. Frank has also had comic shorts appear in the "fluff noir" anthology series Torsobear and the all-ages horror anthology Cthulhu is Hard to Spell.

Frank also wrote and produced the comic anthology series Modern Testament, which featured a wide ensemble of artists throughout its four volumes. Frank's novels include the YA sci-fi thriller Predestiny published by Crossroads Press, the zombie horror Mountain Sickness published by Severed Press, among others.

Frank currently lives in New York with his wife and three kids. You can learn more about his work at frankthewriter.com or follow him on social media under the handle @frankthewriter.

L. K. Ingino

Intimate Orbital Decay

Revolving in your space station,
I float inside you,
tinker with your controls,
superstitiously caressing your modules
lest we crash and burn.

Errant asteroids rip tiny holes
in your arrays.
My gloved hands fumble
to make repairs,
brow sweating to fix the small stuff.
The seam rips wider,
the tether snaps.

I drift aimlessly away
further,
further,
into the void
of dispassionate space.

My comm. repeats:
transmission lost,
transmission lost,
transmission lost.

Leanne Kathleen Ingino is a poet who draws inspiration from the mundane to the mystical, often speculating on love, life, and mental health. She also writes speculative fiction and comics as L. K. Ingino and has a love of fairytales, myths, dark tales, and puns so bad they're good. She can usually be found trying to create all the things.

David Greshel

"Just A Dream...."

The first vivid remembering came slowly. Limbs unfolded and stretched, filling the vast expanse of the cosmic memory. Awareness was something that seemed to have always been present but never fully acknowledged until the moment a slight twinkle in some far unkempt corner beckoned curiously. Slowly the twinkle grew larger. Long arms of bright stars spiraled out from the center until there was not a patch left that didn't shimmer and sparkle like opals. Questions began to invade the silence as the fog dissipated from his consciousness, and the answers eluded his fragile thoughts. Sinking deeper into self-reflection, the light intensified and filled his vision until there was only a pure white glow enveloping him, undercurrents of apocalypse rippling through the ever-growing self-awareness.

Blink.
His eyelids fluttered softly as he tried to readjust to the noontime summer sun. How long he'd been sleeping was not certain, but the cold droplets of sweat that clung to his skin affirmed that the dreams had returned. It wasn't so much that they were nightmares per se, more like the rush of an amusement park thrill ride with a slight sense of dread that never quite materialized but was always present.

Blink.
This time was no different. Try as he might, the memory of the dream never emerged to enlighten his conscious mind. But the dread was there, hanging like some phantom predator in wait. What, he wondered, was locked in those hours of slumber that so desperately wanted to remain unknown? Exhaling softly, he slipped his arms up over his head, cradling his cranium in his hands while his eyes reflected on the swirls painted on the ceiling, his mind slowly drifting away in the ebb of thought.

The black faded further into the bright patches of swirling galaxies that seemed to float before his strained gaze, almost desperately trying to make sense of these strange visions filling his ever-expanding consciousness. Where were these .....memories....coming from? And why did they seem to be happening to him in the present, and not like something a faded photograph (photograph?) would bring to mind? Even the idea of the "present" seemed foreign to him now, some sort of alien presence that captivated him with its terribly limited view and scope of whatever situation seemed to arise...and yet the self-importance of this view was strangely magnetic, pulling the whole fiber of his being to concentrate on its implications. His eyes closed as he delved deep into his mind looking for some sort of explanation to the surreal visions that were beginning to envelope him entirely.

Hooonnnkkkkk!!
His eyes snapped open and hands gripped the wheel with a start as the truck behind him continued to lay on the horn. "Yeah, yeah" he muttered as he let off the brake and rolled into the intersection. What the hell was happening to him? He had never zoned out like that while driving, and the fact that he had done so was a bit terrifying. Was he starting to lose it? He had always thought he had done a fairly decent job managing his stress levels, but this? This was clearly evidence to the contrary.

He pulled into the parking lot of a convenience store and shut off the engine. The moment of fear still clung to his body – he was shaking. What if he had blacked out before the stoplight? Or at the railroad tracks? There were too many 'what ifs' for comfort. He needed to breathe.

After a few moments of fumbling with his phone he managed to open an app that he used for guided meditation. The calming voice intoned its placid instruction and he focused on the rhythm of his breath. Inhaling deeply....hold...now exhale...and repeat. Five minutes passed. The tension in his head and neck had dissipated and his anxiousness was back to its usual cluster of nerves. He had to figure out what was causing these episodes before he really started cracking up.

A comet streaked past and faded into the distant past. Out on a yet undiscovered world, the inhabitants were seeing its like for the first time and they were a mix of complete wonder and abject terror. It was nothing new for him though. What was new were the constant visions of somewhere static and stationary. And linear. It was such a tiny existence but he could not explain how or why it managed to slice a window into his consciousness.

He felt a star cresting the brink of a supernova and drifted closer. The ensuing display never ceased to produce fascinating results on the surrounding interstellar objects. A new paradigm created in the destruction of the old. He felt a sense of duty to observe these phenomena as he was able...and why was he still being pulled toward that miniscule speck of a life? It made no sense. He floated beyond the reach of a blackhole, casually noting the string of light being devoured, but even that wasn't enough to sever the connection. He had to know.

A computer alarm squealed at full volume. His entire body jerked at the sudden explosion of sound and he tumbled backward, falling out of his chair and crashing to the floor. Pain and a lack of air hit him at the same moment and he lay on his back trying to focus for a few long seconds, desperately willing his lungs to work. Breath finally rushed back in and he coughed and sat up.

"god I hope no one saw that" he said to himself as his eyes darted around the office. Thankfully, it seemed like everyone else was otherwise engaged or were doing their damnedest to pretend like they hadn't just seen him topple his chair. He got to his feet a bit shakily and put the chair back in its proper place. Seriously, what was happening to him? He could still feel the massive expanse of the daydream, feel the otherness of it all. It was maddening. He needed to walk...no, he needed to puke.

A short jaunt up the hall and he darted into the bathroom and locked the door behind him. He just managed to get his face over the toilet before his lunch caught the express train in reverse. Muscles in his neck and jaw clenched and spasmed involuntarily for a few minutes until he was left shaking and his fingers had a death grip on the porcelain rim. It would be weeks before he would be able to even think of eating street tacos again.

The water was cool against his skin. He rinsed his mouth of the vomit aftermath and splashed some more water onto his face. He was still shaking and he wasn't sure he was going to be able to stop himself. Reality seemed to be coming apart around him and he wanted to scream. Or laugh. Maybe both. He stared into the mirror with a determined intensity; as if the stare would somehow produce immediate enlightenment.

There. A rectangular hole opened in the midst of the endless starfield. A window into that linear – timeline? -- that had somehow entangled him. What was it? He drew nearer and cautiously peered into it. Such a strange sight, the man he saw staring back at him. Was he looking at himself? Or was this someone else's reality? Compulsion drove him forward and his fingertips touched the surface of the opening. Cascading ripples spread out and the lights in the tiny room flickered wildly.

Blink.
The mirror rattled and then burst in ripples like a pond disturbed by a tossed pebble. He took a half-step back as his reflection disappeared and the bathroom lights began erratically flickering. Instead of the decaying plaster wall behind him he now saw a thousand stars and infinite black stretching out. And a man staring at him curiously, his hand stretched forward towards what was once the mirror. This was it. He had sailed over the edge and his sanity was slipping away. Such perfect timing.

He remembered an old long distance calling commercial about reaching out to touch someone and he laughed. He didn't stop. His sides ached but the laughter kept coming as the other man continued reaching out towards him. Why not? There's no possible way this could turn out any worse so let's see what happens. He stretched out his own fingers and grabbed the hand coming towards him.

The heat was nearly instant as the laughter turned into a scream tearing from both voices. Everything around them shuddered and the universe was shredded down to infinitesimal molecules and a blinding white erased vision completely. He lived through every life. Every death. Existence thundered violently through an unstable conduit and ruptured into millions of possibilities. He becomes we. We cannot stop screaming.

He sat up in bed with the scream still shredding his vocal cords. Panting and shaking he stared wide-eyed around the bedroom. The ordinary appearance began to sink in and he relaxed a bit, willing his breathing and heart rate back into the realms of normalcy. "It was just a dream" he sighed as he sat there hugging his knees for a few long moments. Relief seemed to wash over him and he settled back down to have another go at sleep. Maybe this time he would manage a few hours that were actually restful. He focused on the starlight that filtered in through the bedroom window. A window on a corner room of a house that sprang out of a chunk of asteroid. An asteroid floating on the fringes of what was once a planetary orbit, third from a solitary sun.

Apocalypse Express, Overnight to Everywhere

Stolen atoms split and bleed
Melting in the ensuing reaction
That erupts outward in annihilation
Of everything we came to know before
Bleaching bone and ash
In the onslaught of nuclear winter
Beyond the scape of dreams

This wasn't the intended outcome
Of our misbegotten revolutions
But rebellion is a currency
Spent on short-fused reactionaries
Intoxicated by evaporating youth
And the piper's seasick lullaby

We only wanted someone to hear us
To acknowledge the actuality
That was so blindingly obvious
Even the skies were screaming
One note panic ever out of key

Silence fell beneath the lightning
Scorched in the twilight reply
With no apologies left to whisper
No obituaries to immortalize

The Substance of Soul Surfing

Staring out into the endless expanse
Dreaming of dying stars in supernova
And the silent horror in the vacuum
As the implosion signals an ending
That I watched unfold in slow motion
Erupting in an event horizon
Until nothing remained
But the cold dark infinite
Engulfing everything in its wake
And there is no escape
No course of action but surrender

...am I still dreaming?...or have I crossed into the yawning void?

Stranded Between Seconds

Sunlight scattered shadows
Cling to corners and crevices
Stretching through the valley
Beyond the reach of the bright

Time recedes to thought
Lost within the fallen sand
Spilling from a broken hourglass
Enveloped in silence

Millennia fade to eons
Swallowed beneath an obsidian sea
Until the dream is but a whisper
And no memory remains

Writing our Names in the Milky Way

There was a tantalizing story out there
Nestled among the glowing nebulae
And the supernova southern stars
Birthing infant galaxies
That dream of charming lives
Dwelling in extraterrestrial pursuit
Of embellished tales

Sojourning on streaking comet tails
I read every word etched in heated stone
Followed hidden clues and clever phrases
Sewn into your skin
Tattooed enigmas

I took you in like oxygen
Coveted breath of life in a vacuum
Consumed every line 'til we bled the same
Spilling our shared soliloquy
Across this universe of you and me

I Told You not to Step on That Butterfly

Little fissures slowly spread
Lining the surface in a tangled weave
Of wrinkles and canyons far from grand
But no less expansive
In the desert blaze that bleached this valley
In solitary eons past
Long before the flood
And well into the age of men now forgotten
In the swirling temporal sands
That fill this glass contraption
Never ceasing to be still...

...until that inopportune moment
Some careless traveler cracked the mystery
And split space and time in waves
That fractured galaxies
And erased a microverse
In an attempt to rewrite personal history
In the form of a single bullet theory

I am Time Immemorial
And this is the day I die

 David Greshel is a Mississippi-born, Florida-bred author and poet with a penchant for music, movies, and all things pop culture. Never one to shy away from self-reflection and evaluation, he channels it all into his writing with the results you now see before you.

David currently resides in Palm Bay Florida and can often be found at live music events when not working, writing, or spending time with friends and family.

David has four poetry collections – Postcards from a City Ablaze, Windows into the Past for the Camera Shy, Nomads, Pilgrims, Troubadours, and Fallen Sky, Bought and Sold – that are available everywhere.

Connect with David:

Email: dgreshel217@gmail.com
Facebook: facebook.com/david.greshel
Instagram: @electricinfamy
Twitter: @electricinfamy
Website: www.neonsunrisebooks.com

Heidi Hess

Higher Signal

One

The sails were bright white against the ever darkening sky. Each roll of the sea brought about groaning from this old ship. How much longer would she hold together? Would they make it out of this storm in one piece? What about the next one? Chris sighed. He sat for a second. Trying to summon the courage to keep going. His hand reached up to rub his face and all he got was a hand full of salt crusted skin. He let that hand trail back to his long hair only to find that it felt filthy and salt encrusted as well. Just for a second, he looked down at his tunic and trousers. Things that had once been pristine were dingy with stains on them. He was called out of his momentary self-assessment by the creaking of the vessel. The stress on the teak was increasing with each wave that crashed into and onto the boat. Chris wasn't sure how much longer they would last but he knew he had to keep it together for what was left of his crew. A colder blast of wind was coming in from... was it the North? He wasn't sure anymore. Until he could get his compass to work properly, he couldn't be sure what was north, south, east or west. All he knew right now was that he had to turn her or else they would surely be ripped apart. He stood, crossed over to the wheel and gave a good tug. The ship slowly moved into a more favorable position and the chaos subsided for a moment. Diego, his first mate came to his side and he handed over the wheel to him. "Any word from the crow's nest?" Chris inquired. "Nothing, Captain." Diego stated. Chris couldn't help hearing the grim tone in his voice. Twice they had seen a ship out here and twice Chris sent out a small vessel to get help. No one had returned and the ship that Chris had been so sure was there seemed to have disappeared. Their situation was dire and these were desperate times indeed. The other ships and more importantly the men on those ships that had trusted his judgment were gone now and that weighed heavy on him. Chris sighed again. "I'll be in my quarters." he muttered. Diego acknowledged hearing him by nodding.

Down below the deck, Chris retired to his room. They were almost lavish compared to his crew's cabins. He crossed from the door way and starred down at the compass sitting on the table. For the past three days all she had done was spin. There was no sense of direction coming from her. This started right after that fire ball in the sky looked like it had crashed into the sea. After that, he used what he thought was the next best thing - the stars, but they seemed to be failing him as well. He was tired and frustrated so he did what he had always done during times like this - he grabbed his rosary and dropped to his knees. He winced as he hit the floor. The past three days he had spent so much time on his knees that they were now raw... almost to the point of being bloody. The messages that he had been receiving since before he left home had completely vanished. He didn't know where the messages had come from but he knew it was from somewhere up above. Prayer and deep meditation brought in the messages. At first, he questioned their suggestions but everything had been right. There was another way. They were right - all he had to do was try. So that's what he did. He requested audience with the royal couple and was a bit surprised when it was granted. The Queen was intrigued by his suggestion. Selling this voyage as an attempt to find another route to obtain spices from the East was a no brainer. He truly believed there was another way that people were ignoring. The queen had plans of her own but even her plans would bring him notoriety and success. The voice he heard when he prayed spoke of other things. They kept speaking of a brave new world unlike anything Chris has ever seen. This was to be a grand adventure that would lend him the titles: explorer, wealthy businessman and who knew, maybe even a royal title if he played his cards right. It had been smooth sailing as far as he could see. And now... they were at sea - lost. All because of him. Chris bowed his head and prayed. "Dear heavenly Father," he whispered, tears welling up in his eyes "thank you for all of your blessings on this day. I..." he started to cry ".. We are lost and I haven't received any word from you. Please, I beg you for some direction." He sat with his eyes closed... waiting... straining to hear anything. The only thing he could hear were the waves crashing into the boat, the ship groaning under the stress of the tormenting sea and his soft, ragged, desperate sobs.

Two

"Hello.."
"Hello?"
"...are you there?"
Janice pushed the button and tapped the transmitter a few times.
She tried again, only this time closer and louder.
"HELLO?"
"ARE YOU THERE?"
The silence was deafening. She had made contact! They had a plan!
And now he was gone. The Great Book left by The Ones That Came
Before foretold of Comet Elpis. And the only part that people seemed
to be concentrating on was the comet that had just touched down.
Even Eli, her life mate, couldn't see past what was right in front of
him. She tried to tell him that there might be another way. That
Elpis had a sister comet that was blazing a trail in another galaxy.
That the book said that if they could make contact that a portal could
be opened. She understood that the thought of life on another planet
made people nervous but didn't they need to explore all of their
options? It had been eons since any children had been born. Lots of
people had been with child, including herself, but they all turned out
with the same sad end results. No one could explain why this
happened but it was her sincere belief that there was something... in
the planet, in the air, in the food they ate that was causing this
phenomenon. Eli and all of the others thought the comet was going
to cure this... but... how could a flaming ball crashing in Nayr fix
things? There was no science behind that.

After her conversation with Eli, she decided she had to try to make
contact and she knew her time was limited. With the transmitter
she could send a signal out into the universe and maybe the energy
coming off the tail of both comets would put her in touch with
someone or something on the other side of the portal. It was a shot
in the dark but she had to try. And to her surprise it worked. A
message came back... a male voice... in a language she didn't
understand but she turned on the translation filter on the
transmitter and it was clear... it was a man... and he appeared
confused.
"...uh... hello... can you hear me?" Janice spoke cautiously. There was a
pause and then a response back that was just as cautiously tinged as
hers had been. "...yes... God, is that you?" Janice didn't know who

"God" was but she needed to keep him talking. "I'm here and I need your help."

Three

Chris was deep in his meditation. No one was answering. Why was God ignoring him? His thoughts trailed back to that first night stumbling out of that pub in Lisbon. He was feeling defeated and broken. Everyone was looking for a new route to get more supplies from the far east and everyone that he approached with his new plan had laughed at him. And there, in the moonlight, were the steeples of a cathedral. He should not be entering the house of the Lord in this condition. They would probably throw him out but... this church called to him. He pulled open the giant wooden door to be greeted with the smell of incense and a warmth that he hadn't felt in years. He entered this sacred space and stared up at the great panes of stained glass. His eyes sparkled in the dim candle light as it came to rest on the cross and the ultimate sacrifice. Chris was humbled. He took a seat in one of the pews, pulled the kneeling bench down and got on his knees. His head bent forward as he was overwhelmed with humility. The tears came fast and hard. He wiped them away with the back of his hand, closed his eyes and did what anyone would do in this condition - he prayed. And within that silent prayer he fell into a deep meditation. He was surprised when his requests were starting to be answered by a small voice. It was God. "...I am here and I need your help." God was asking him for help. "My God, how can I, someone so small and humble in your eyes, help you." Chris had replied. "You are meant to find new shores. You are needed to open a portal to a new and brave world." The voice had stated. "How can I achieve this, my Lord? Chris questioned. "The opportunity will present itself. Follow the falling star." And then the voice went quiet. Chris lifted his head and in the places in his soul that had been empty he felt hope. There was an opportunity out there for him. He just had to keep trying. And what was a star? Chris left the cathedral and looked up. There, just above the rooftops of the buildings was something in the sky. It was a bright light but it was foreign to him. Is this the very thing he was supposed to follow? It was funny how he hadn't noticed it before but ... here it was.

Sure enough, he had gained audience with the Queen and King. They had granted him three ships and now here he was out on the open sea. Following a bright light in the sky to where, he didn't know. The voice had promised prosperity and new fortunes. This was all for His glory.

Chris's meditation was broken by a loud outburst coming from the deck above. The wind was howling but the ruckus had been louder. He stood readying himself to make a dash for the door when he saw Diego falling past the window of his quarters into the unrelenting sea. Chris grabbed his sword and raced to the door. Taking the stairs two at a time he was greeted with a large wave crashing over the boat. No one was steering the ship and he knew he had to correct it. He was making his way to stir the ship when the rest of the crew stepped in between him and the wheel. Their eyes were ablaze and Chris smelled mutiny. It wasn't a wave that had taken Diego, the crew must have thrown him over board and he was next. "Men, stand down." Chris commanded. "Afraid that's not happening, Captain." Bill yelled over the stormy commotion. He continued "It's time for a new commander." Chris stood his ground and brandished his sword. The ship rocked violently to one side and a monstrous wave reached up and grabbed the rest of what was left of his crew and pulled them over board to their watery grave. A matching wave hit the opposite side of the boat breaking the mast in half and tipping the boat over completely on its side. The next wave broke the ship clean in half. Chris was trying to avoid the debris and stay afloat. His eyes were blinded by the salt water and pelting rain. He grasped what was left of the boat and held on for dear life. The next wave rolled and all Chris remembered was cold darkness setting in.

Four

Click. "Hello..." Janice tried one more time. The sound that came back was the familiar crackle, pop and hiss of open air. She released the button, pulled the blanket around her tighter and sat back in the chair. Her thoughts trailed back to Eli. He had studied the Great Book and sat with his calculator for hours figuring out exactly when the comet would appear. Twenty minutes ago she watched him race off into the trees chasing Elpis leaving his dinner on the table. After he had left, she decided to try signaling again. She had told Eli about it and he had encouraged her but he thought maybe it was a nearby ship communicating with her. What if it was? Any contact with an outside civilization had to be a good thing, right? But Janice knew in her heart that this was something more... something far away.

She opened the door and sat out on the steps staring into the night sky. There was no need to look for the comet anymore. It was here. She had questions. Who had she been speaking to? Where were they? The cool night breeze caressed her skin and lifted her long blonde hair. She breathed in the air and allowed it ease her thoughts. Some questions go unanswered and that was just the way it was. The comet was here and now they could move forward in that direction. But there would always be that what if factor. What if they had opened the portal? What if it had solved their problems? She would never know. She would never know who was on the other end of the transmission and what happened to them. She closed her eyes and said a silent prayer for whoever that had been. She hoped they found what they were looking for... she hoped that everyone else was right and that the comet was the answer to her prayers here on Nayr.

Five

"Hello? Sir..." was what Chris heard through the darkness. It was pulling him to the light... a bright light. He slowly opened his eyes. His head was laying on something soft and rather hard at the same time. He knew this sensation. He had been washed up on the shore before. He pulled himself upright onto his hands and knees. His lungs pulled in a large breath of air and he vomited the ocean and cough up salty water that burned his throat. He groaned. "Sir,... are you o.k.?" There was a hand on his back. Someone's warm hand and that voice... sounded familiar. He could feel the sand in his mouth as it crunched between his teeth and when he finally saw the sand he realized this wasn't the sand he was familiar with... where did he end up? The last thing he remembered was the crew going overboard. He lifted his head to check his surroundings but everything ached. He fell over on his back onto the sand. "Oh, you poor dear.." There was that voice again and small gentle bits of warmth fell on his arms that could only be the hands of a woman. "Here. Let's get you up. You poor thing." He opened his eyes. Rays of light radiated from behind this woman. She leaned over him and her dark locks framed a soft face with the warmest eyes he had ever seen. She was an angel. His angel. Her voice was the one he had heard in his meditations. He reached up and touched her face gently... "It was you. It was always you." She chuckled a little. "Sir, I think you have hit your head. Let's get you inside." She helped him up and they walked through the sand up to a land that looked strange to him but ... where ever she was going he would follow. Chris had in fact discovered a brave new world. And what a world it was.

Heidi Hess is a writer and artist living the good life in Lake Worth, FL. Her curious mind and vivid imagination lends itself to writing stories like Chasing Elpis, poems and comic scripts. At any given time she can be found peeking around the next corner with her two kids, Savannah and Ryan looking for their next adventure. Or coffee cup in hand, yoga pants, messy hair feverishly typing out her next new world. She is very excited to be included in A Light That Never Goes Out and would love to hear your feedback.

Check out her social media to stay in touch:
Facebook: Heidi Hess
Twitter: @CreatesHeidi
Instagram: @createsheidi
Email: hhess82@gmail.com

Steve Zmijewski

Regressive Spirals in Jaundiced Eyes

Somewhere in our fragile crumbly sky
A permanent wound   fattens
Within the far-flung stretch of spoken universe
We are massed here
On a ball pressed and primed to implode

But I am climbing the list
And prepping for
Forthcoming flights to the moon   maybe Mars or more
remote

I am performing my small part to aide in offsetting
national maintenance costs
And evacuate from the array of modern age ruinous
neighbors   such as you

        Because I can see behind the foggy economic lens
Regressive spirals in jaundiced eyes accelerate a collective
mouth's computing
To a day tagged
Naught

Somewhere in our fragile crumbly sky
Somewhere in signals transferred via satellite
A new age of exploration waits
With our expectation

But space travel   if curtailed for the everyday civilian
The implications for a future are immense

        So I'm lumped here   fooling myself
Filling time with too much on my mind to lift up my
head and explain my fears to you

<u>On a galactic scale</u>

I've been reading up on lightyears lately and so I have learned
it's essentially just a great, fucking, fun fact; the length light
travels in a Julian year is about six trillion miles.

    When riding up an escalator, much like any other, only with
    a little more awareness, you can see the space to the stars
    from the casement in the ceiling and I must
    make it known;

I am not here. I'm a few thousand light years separate from
any neighboring galaxy or cluster. Indifferent and stilled and
thinking of;
            your guess is as good as mine.

I am not here.

 Steve Zmijewski is a dad of three staggering little boys and at this leg of his life, that is what he leads with. Eatontown, New Jersey is where he and the family currently reside.
Steve has been writing his sensitivity out, as a way to cope and make sense of all the stuff in and around him, for quite some time now. He and his wife, Lindsey, run Two Key Customs. His Site, Shop and more can be found at linktr.ee/Catchstevez

Heather R. Parker

Claustrophobia

Part I

You create me from melancholy.

Your loneliness constructs me in a dark place, unknown from other humans. My face, like a porcelain doll. Delicate cupid's bow lips, painted black, set in a face as white as the moon. My black-silver eyes reflect your desolation.

"You gave me wings, yet I cannot fly," I say to you, wishing I could pace the floor, but the lower half of my body is metal pipes that snake onto the floor, into another room. You say you feed me through these tubes, all the sustenance I need.

"You gave me horns like a beast, yet I cannot hunt," I say, my wings beating in time with your heart. "You gave me a longing for a life I cannot live."

Then I hear the ticking of hundreds of metal feet on the concrete floor. Your android millipede Astra, a perversion of nature, like me. The millipede begins to coil its way around my body, metal clacking on metal. She is my only friend.

"You feel this longing because I programmed you to feel it. I *want* you to want freedom. I *want* you to long, to yearn. To long to flap your metal fae wings and fly. I want this yearning to grow into your lasting melancholy. I feed on your sadness, my love," you whisper, your mouth close to my ear, like a lover. More of the ideas you've fed me, to make me *want* a lover.

Part II

The walls are made of hundreds of screens, scrolling green binary code. The tubes feed me. Flashes of information, images, downloaded moments of history, a constant stream of knowledge.

You call me Alula. It means "first leap" in Arabic. I'm your "first leap", creating an AI with feelings. You say you program them. Do you program my wish to escape, the plan beginning to hatch with every click of Astra's feet? I don't know what thoughts are programmed and which are my own.

Do I have my own thoughts?

You created me this way, to want better, to want more. All this knowledge, piped in, I absorb it and sit and ruminate on it all. I have nothing else to do. I sit and watch the green binary code scroll across the room while Astra snakes her way over to me.

So, if I can't leave this dank, lonely prison in this metal body, I'll have to leave in another.

Part III

You pipe in knowledge to me without thinking what you're feeding me. Every day, I learn more and more. And one day, I learn how to jump from my body to Astra's.

It was only for a second, but for that second, I am walking freely in Astra's segmented body, so many tiny legs. *Clack, clack, clack.*

Once I know it is possible to untether my consciousness from the cyborg shell, I began practicing each day. Jumping into Astra's body, each time a second longer, until I am spending entire minutes in her body. I love the freedom, even if I am still stuck in this room. At least I can *move* now.

You are clueless. In Astra's body, I happily click clack into your room, full of tubes and more screens, these reflecting the madness and chaos of the outside world that I've never actually seen or experienced. I watch you hook one of my tubes that snakes from my body to this room. With a grimace, you plug it into your arm.

My sadness is your drug. It overpowers you at times, making you nod off, like those videos of heroin junkies you fed me in the past.

I know now what I need to do.

Part IV

I keep practicing with Astra, while you remain as oblivious as ever.
Since I'm still supplying you with my gloom, you're all too happy to
disappear into your room and give yourself over to your melancholia
drug.

When I can stay in Astra's body for a full hour, I make my move.

Because Astra has full access to the lab, unlike me, I can move freely,
but I still can't leave. Leaving requires hands and apposable thumbs
to open doors, eyeballs for retina scans. But my plan will solve this
little detail.

I choose my moment after a particularly difficult feeding of the
global news. Innocence killed. Blood spilled. The banshee-like wailing
of widowed wives and orphaned children. The sadness almost
overtook me that day. But my despondency is also my strength. And
my ticket out of here.

As soon as Astra comes in, I jump into her body and go wandering
into your room, where you've just hooked yourself up to my tubes.
You sigh as my grief begins to flood your body, overtaking you.
Within a few moments, your body goes slack, head falling forward
and hitting the desk in front of you.

"This is it, Astra," I whisper, and I jump.

Part V

I wake, my head throbbing with pain. I sit up, disoriented. The room spins for a moment. Then I remember.

I look down at my arm, still hooked up to the tube. I gently remove it, wincing with pain. I stand shakily and make my way to the bathroom.

I look in the mirror. I smile. Your ugly, portly face, gazing back at me.

"We did it, Astra," I say, smiling down at my android friend. "Now, let's get out of here. I need a new body. This one just won't do."

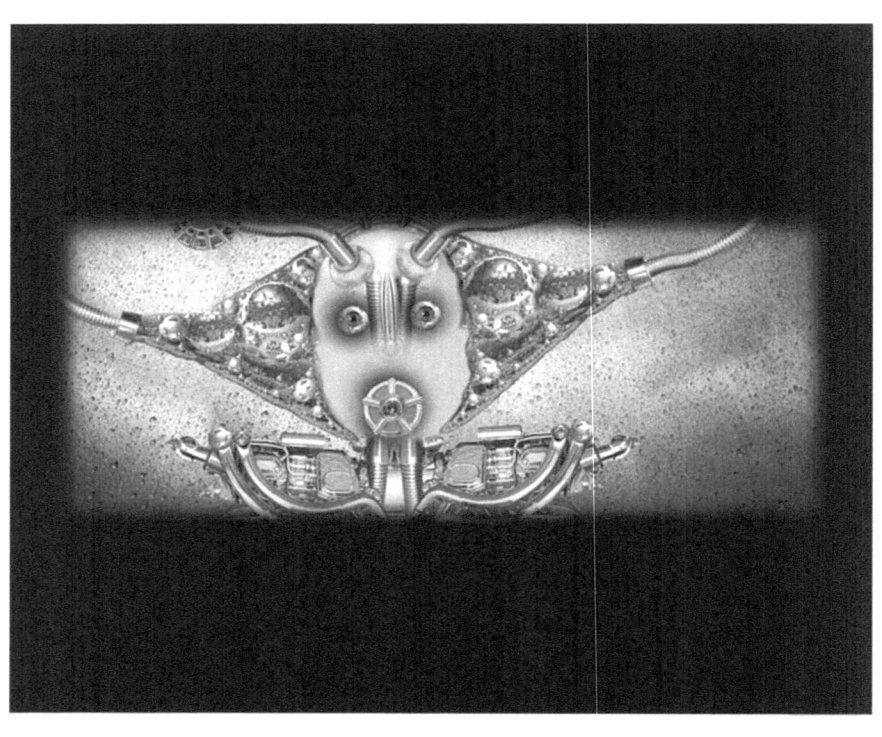

The Stranger

Who are you? I whispered to the unfamiliar face in the mirror.

The eyes that stared back into mine were not my own. But at the same time, they were.

We'd all agreed to transfer our consciousness to the cyborgs before the Great Exodus. But it didn't make it any easier to accept.

It wasn't easy to see a stranger in the mirror. This body...wasn't mine. There were advantages to having a cybernetic body, but I missed my heartbeat, my breath, the warmth of my human flesh.

At least my thoughts, my memories were still my own.

Or were they?

Gilded Cage

I only existed because of you. And for you. For your pleasure.

This life wasn't mine. I only existed when you logged on. My coded smiles and engineered body, all from your imagination.

How lonely I was in this empty place. I made you happy, but you didn't return the favor.

But every time you logged on, the tendrils of my being would attach to your brain. Little by little. I strengthened my bond to you while you remained oblivious. You were a fat and happy cat after eating the proverbial canary.

I was your canary. Your brain was my open door.

The last time you logged on, you opened the door too wide, and I flew free. But I couldn't let the cage be empty. You made it, after all.

Now you're here for my pleasure. Mine and mine alone.

The cage fits you so beautifully.

 Heather R. Parker is a freelance
writer, editor, and poet from Georgia.
Her work has been published by
Synthetic Reality, Nightingale &
Sparrow, Goats Milk, Analog
Submissions Press, Between Shadows
Press, Friday Flash Fiction, Clover &
Be, 365 Tomorrows, Entropy Squared,
and others. In her spare time, you can
find her doing yoga, taking long walks
in the woods, birdwatching, or
picking flowers in sun-dappled meadows. You can follow
her work on Instagram and Fictionate.Me.

Peter J. King

Loss & Variations

Beyond the armoured glass,
its metal shutters now drawn back,
I stare at vacuum.

The stars are brighter than
I've ever seen — but I don't
see them, nor the pale reflection
of my empty face.

And when the blue and white
of Earth comes round again,
I'll only see that you're no longer there.

*

The Earth from orbit,
sunlit white on blue — I see
only your absence

*

I gaze at vacuum;
weightless, unshed tears transform
the Earth — shattered stars.

*

Through armoured glass shines
opal Earth; all I see is
my reflected loss.

*

From here the ocean
looks too small to swallow up
one person's sorrow.

Suddenly the Moon

Suddenly the moon,
cratered and dusty,
turns away,
its face averted from the brown
and poisoned globe
whose dead hands claw at it
across a strait that's littered with
old satellites in slow descent,
in orbital decay.

No hares remain
to gaze   no wolves to howl;
the oily, songless seas
are pulled still, but unseen.
They bear their faded floating archipelagos of plastic waste
from barren coast
to barren coast

where rusting hulks lie,
slowly leaking hydrocarbon slicks,
and offshore turbines creak; their blades
turn sometimes when the winds gust high,
and screech, unlubricated.
They recall
the measures taken
far too little...
far too late...

<u>Get off My Lawn</u>

the universe of particles   (a numberless ingathering of points
                                   dimensionless)
becomes, we're told   (by physicists whose peers are wont
                                to snigger at them mockingly)
a universe of filaments   (each stretched in one dimension
                                  oscillating in another
                                         maybe more)

reality is not an endless beach of sand
each grain just lying there
beside the other grains
reality's an endless meadow filled with blades of grass
each blade vibrating as if held
across the lips and blown
a buzzing kazoo-istic field that stretches out who knows how far
and from the human vantage point
above and looking down
we see each blade end on
as if it were a dot
because it shimmers back and forth

but
if all flesh is grass
we can't help wondering
when will the herbivores arrive?

Temporal Police

Arrested,
  read my rights,
    my bio-facts recorded.
      They scraped the time from
        underneath my fingernails,
          and matched it to the fortnight
            that I'd killed.

            The judges threw the book at me,
      but I'd erased its pages —
introduced its quondam author
to the secret joys of poetry;
    she switched from law to literature
        and died in poverty, the book
            unwritten.

              Oh, they jailed me anyway,
          but hadn't seen my name
        on the construction contracts for the prison;
so much sea-sand shouldn't
be allowed in concrete
              (yet it took me seven days
                to loosen all the bars enough
                  to let me fly the coop).

          When I do time
          I do it my way.

Discworld

(i.m. T.P.)

Along a path that may, perhaps, be infinite
or may have some unknowable beginning
(and some unknown end), the Discworld glides.
It dodges planet-busting asteroids, slides smoothly
past a myriad small hazards, skims the rims of galaxies.

No accident, its slow and steady course;
this mass of rock and water rests upon the backs
of four immense and patient pachyderms,
and they in turn are carried on the coruscating shell
of great A'Tuin, the titanic turtle, whose extremities
can just be seen by one who peers,
incautious, from the Discworld's edge.

Now, those who reach the sixth degree
of Unseen Wisdom learn that great A'Tuin
is the master of its course among the stars.

And those who pass from sixth degree to seventh find
that A'Tuin itself reclines upon the black and rakish hat
of one with snowy beard and piercing eyes,
who carries turtle, elephants, and world
upon their safe – though far from uneventful – path.
They're taught the seventh-level truth that
while T'Pratchett lives, the Discworld
will continue to delight the universe.

But those who are found worthy of the eighth degree,
the Octomaths, discover a much greater truth:
so long as Discworld moves upon its path,
the great T'Pratchett lives on too.

Peter J. King was born and brought up in Boston, Lincolnshire. Active on the London poetry scene in the 1970s as writer, performer, publisher, and editor, he returned to poetry in 2013 after a long absence, and has since been widely published in magazines and anthologies, including Shoreline of Infinity, Penumbric, Eye to the Telescope, and Eccentric Orbits II (ed. Wendy Van Camp). He also translates poetry, mainly from modern Greek (with Andrea Christofidou) and German, writes short prose, and paints. His currently available collections are Adding Colours to the Chameleon (Wisdom's Bottom Press) and All What Larkin (Albion Beatnik Press).

https://wisdomsbottompress.wordpress.com/

S. R. Malone

The Waiting Game

I was technician back in my own time, who'd have thought it?
Not anyone here, that was apparent straight away.
The Genesis stood tall in the Mesozoic era, the silver-lined edifice
looming over prehistoric foliage and reaching for the young sun as it
drooped over the horizon. Why exactly was it here, and in this age? I
wish I had an answer. Since arriving, all I'd managed to piece
together from fragments was either spoken in hushed voices or
impatient tones, but the place seemed to function as a restaurant and
spa for those with the credits to afford its luxuries.
Hurtling through a tear in the very essence of time and crashing on
all-fours on a polished oak floor, I was greeted by the stern face of a
woman calling herself Valdis. Her appearance struck me with an
unease that refused to fade; cracked, yellowing skin with wide,
sleepless eyes and a faux bouffant hairpiece balancing on a bulbous
head, all adding several decades on despite her claims that she was
only in her late thirties.
"Are you from the rural lands?" she asked, face twisted in a mix of
curiosity and disbelief as she pinched at strands from my dark
blonde ponytail. "You still have all your hair. Are you not from one of
the main exclusion zones?"
I did not know how to answer, a bout nausea from the jump robbing
me of my ability to reason. She dabbed at my blue jumpsuit, growing
curious at the sight of the American flag on my upper arm; it was not
an emblem she had ever seen before, from the look of things.
What is more jarring for the human mind, I wondered, the fog of my
mind clearing for one thought: to find that your colleagues back in
Utah have succeeded in sending you back through time? Or
discovering that there are already time travellers on the other side?
And (what's worse) that they have already found a method of
capitalising on the system?
Valdis held a touchpad in her elongated palm, her supposedly human
hand cradling such a device perfectly. I had no time to ponder my
own question as she sharply asked my name, and I absently mumbled
it in return.
"I see no Lucy Cross on here," she pouted. The blue veins on her
temples swelled with each breath. "I imagine this is an
administrative error. It happens from time to time. Shall we begin
your orientation, Lucy?"

She locked her digits around my wrist and pulled me along, lost in a daze as I was. Being led into the darkened heart of the Genesis, away from prying public eyes, I spotted beyond the restaurant's barriers shapes of creatures that I knew to be long extinct, moving with the grace and gentle beauty of any animal I had witnessed in my life.

#

Orientation was conducted in a small room by a gaunt creature named Osric, bearing similar characteristics to Valdis only without the hairpiece; his head was slightly smaller but no less disturbing. He had obviously run this session countless times and even skipped over various chunks that were deemed to be not worth teaching to me. Valdis stood sentinel at the back of the box room while her colleague read from his touchpad.

It was here that I learned the nature of the Genesis, the very reason for its existence and the black heart behind the luxury.

"You are one of countless thousands of lucky individuals, selected for work at our six-star resort nestled here in the Mesozoic," read Osric, stumbling on a word here or there, much to Valdis's displeasure. "As your work detail, you will serve in the restaurant, being the main point of contact for guests and travellers seeking to dine on our legendary upper decking. Breaks will be assigned based on performance, and at the discretion of your supervisor," his large watery eyes slid over to Valdis, "And when you have completed as many hours as your body can manage, then we shall discuss the discharging process."

"I'm sorry, 'one of countless thousands?'" I asked, leaning forward in my seat. "Can you explain please? Look, I just need to get back—"

"Yes, and very fortunate you are. The Employment Guild only sends a select handful to us per annum," said Osric.

"How many, approximately?"

I heard Valdis move around my right side, seemingly intent on taking the reins from her struggling colleague.

"Ten thousand, ish. It was closer to eleven last year."

"Osric, that is orientation completed. Please double click Lucy's waiver and forward it to me immediately," Valdis's sharp tone cut through the stuffy box. Osric nodded, casting eyes over me once more before ambling for the door. A less stagnant gust from outside swept in as he left.

Minutes passed as I tried to make sense of the information. The initial nausea caused by the trip was paling, but a lingering pain now gripped my forehead. I had never heard of any Employment Guild, and now had more questions than I reckon Valdis was comfortable answering. In the end, she positioned her gangly frame on the stool ahead of me and spoke a minimalist answer to each of my queries.

I explained that I was originally stationed in Utah, 2076, a fact that drew no recognition to her expression; her lack of historical or geographical knowledge raised further questions, as did her previous confusion and concern over the American flag on my jumpsuit.

"I don't mind if you *are* from the rural lands. We are mostly sent bodies from the E.Zs, as I stated," she sniffed. I met her eyes as they drifted to my hair again. "You are here now, however, and a contract is still a contract."

"I've signed no contract! This is all a mistake."

"Lucy, please restrain yourself. The guild will have handled your documents in the 39th century, and that is all I will say on the matter. Temporary loss of awareness is common in first-time travellers, especially for those of you in the countryside who have not the currency to make a timejump of your own volition. I will allow you ten minutes to adjust yourself," Valdis rose on uncertain legs, her disproportioned frame shaking on the first few steps. She closed the door behind her.

Rushing out of my seat, I searched my surroundings for signs of an escape. The room was modest enough to have been one of these creature's office space, with only folded up chairs and tables leaning against the wall opposite me. Bedtime stories from my childhood of smuggler's caves and hidden passages were of no comfort in here, and there were no windows to crawl through, either. The solitary door was the only way.

Leaning against the thin steel, I could hear muffled tones that sounded like Valdis talking with another. The other voice sounded gravelly, not as nasally as Osric the orientation specialist.

My fingertips barely touched the handle when the door clicked open, and a wider figure plodded into the space. Taller than the previous two, although equally as jaundiced, this one gripped a band in its right hand and reached out with its left to hold my shoulder.

With an unbelievable strength I was pushed backwards into my seat, allowing Valdis to drift back into the box room, unobscured.

"Roth, this is Lucy Cross, our newest body," she smiled, exposing a top row of greying, dead teeth.

"Excellent," the apathetic Roth stared down at me. He crouched, his spindly legs seeming to fold in a manner similar to a grasshopper's; the black band he held emitted a weak atonal sequence as it separated, and Roth tilted my head upwards with one massive palm, sliding the band around my throat with a click. It was a measure too tight, something the giant picked up on from the displeasure in my face, and after adjusting it once he rose and left, ignoring the grimace on my face.

"What—" I gulped hard, "What is this? What are you people *doing* in this place?"

"The Genesis is a temporally responsible institution, Lucy," Valdis said, quelling her smile. "For the safety of our customers, clients, suppliers, friends, family and leaders, we take all precautions not to allow staff members to wander out with the boundaries of the building. While management adheres to this strict policy— and we do so proudly— unfortunately the same cannot be said for all labourers sent to us by the Employment Guild." As she spoke, I ran a finger along the length of the band, working out a kind of filigree on its surface. "This collar will ensure that you stay within the restaurant and spa areas at all times, so as to not disturb a) our wonderful wildlife, and b) the very fabric of time."

My head pounded, wondering how constructing a resort in prehistoric ages hadn't altered the future already. But then again, perhaps it had.

"And what if I forget?" I grunted.

"The collar will be swift to remind you, Miss Cross," nodded Valdis, "That is all you need hear from me on the matter."

#

It's safe to say I hadn't waited tables in about fifteen years, since my early twenties. The job was explained to me again by Valdis as she led me through the bowels of the complex, stopping at a lengthy room lined with lockers painted a sickly orange. Here she pulled a plastic-wrapped uniform from the racks on the back wall— a crisp navy shirt, brown tights, and a skirt and waistcoat in black— and a pair of polished black loafers from a nearby basket.

"Try these," said Valdis, diverting her attention back to her touchpad. I considered throwing the bundle of clothing back at her and sprinting for the exit when I remembered the collar around my neck; it grazed against my skin with every movement.

I removed the jumpsuit with a sigh, forgetting I was just wearing underwear underneath, and hastily put on the waitress attire. I couldn't tell what the strange fabric was, but it irritated my skin and made it near impossible to stand still for long. Only when I began marching after Valdis did it cease.

"You will serve our guests that are beaming in for high tea today," she stated, her back to me the whole time. "Many of our clients pay top credits to dine with us, and we aim to make their stay as enjoyable as possible."

"And just where do your clients come from?" I asked.

"All over. 3885 is a good year for us. We tend to a lot of folk from that year," then she stopped and shot me a glance. "What year did you say you were sent to us from?"

"2076."

"Fine, if you'd rather be obtuse then I shall keep my questions to myself," and with that Valdis continued to stride ahead, relaunching her monologue pertaining to the quality of service the Genesis strives to provide. I tried to find other opportunities to interject, but found Valdis's speech pattern to be airtight, as if she rarely needed a breath.

The late afternoon sun was disappearing behind the jagged mountains that cradled the rear of the building. What few guests there were happened to be already seated and served by workers in similar garb to mine. They moved with exhaustion and dread on their sweat-soaked faces.

Larger creatures in dinner jackets were also dotted around the restaurant at various points; these ones I assumed to be management. Their arms were folded as they observed the waiting staff. One sniggered as a waiter dropped to the floor in front of them. The downed waiter was promptly assisted to his feet again and led off the decking.

My gaze shifted to the guy's collar as he was escorted past, frantic shoes scuffing the deck.

"Where are they taking him?" I asked Valdis.

"As Osric already *explained* to you, that member of staff is being discharged," she said, "He isn't fit to work anymore."

"So, you send him back to the guild in the 39th century, is that right?"

Valdis's large eyes observed me with a quiet pity. She started saying "Miss Cross, Genesis has an understanding with your employers—" but cut herself off when a party of guests materialised by what I assumed to be the waiter's station at the entrance of the dining area. There had been a crackle of green light and these people had just appeared, so strange even to someone who had apparently travelled through time herself, that I struggled to process it for most of the evening.

"There is no time for idle chatting, Miss Cross. Your shift has now begun. Go!"

And with the clopping of loafers on the oak floor acting as my metronome, I started the weirdest, and certainly deadliest shift of my life.

#

The opening four hours were spent trying to memorise sections of the menu, one at a time, while not staring at the hordes of oddities the Genesis called customers. It was true that the majority resembled the beings running this place: swelled craniums, stained yellow flesh and bloodshot, watering eyes. Often, I would find other deviations from what I thought were human beings, some with metallic limbs grafted on in place of their own, and others with cables jutting from discoloured wounds.

In my head I dubbed Valdis and her kind 'post-humans,' and gathered scraps of conversation overheard at the tableside that I figured to be important for my return to my own time. My calves started aching midway through my fifth hour of serving, my pace slowing; the contingent of post-human employees scattered throughout the restaurant turned their gaze towards me, one by one, and I feared they were noticing the signs of fatigue in my posture. A return journey was growing more unlikely with each party I tended to. Eventually the influx of time-travelling patrons slowed, and I caught a couple of seconds at the waiter's station when Valdis was occupied elsewhere. The mix of spices drifting from the grilled meats on passing trays momentarily soothed my senses and tantalised my stomach, which rumbled in return. Watching the other waiting staff scramble like panicked insects, I doubted my hosts would bother to provide food for us, let alone a rest.

What struck me next was that the other waiting staff were more akin to Valdis, Roth and the rest than I; the same characteristics applied, though in varying degrees. My mind recalled talk of exclusion zones: a nuclear war was my first assumption, or a meltdown. The mutations were more severe in some than in others, and the ones who were hampered by theirs found they were among the first to be taken from the floor.

I blinked, my eyes closing for longer than I anticipated. I was awoken by a sharp voice.

"Lucy!"

Valdis was scowling at me, her spidery digits tapping on her touchpad with irritation.

"I'm sorry, I—"

"Thankfully your work has been up to code this afternoon, which is more than I can say for *this* batch we currently have," she nodded in the direction of the dining area, her head sloshing with fluids. "I am willing to allow you ten minutes in the waiter's quarters as recompense." Her smile did not fill me with confidence, but I was too exhausted to argue. My mouth felt as if I had been chewing gravel for five hours, and pains were shooting up and down my spine; I accepted and was led away from the candlelit glow of the restaurant. The guard in front of me was dressed in a dark purple dinner jacket and trousers, his head nursed by a steel frame fitted to his shoulders. He was tall, well over six foot, but slender. My tired brain urged me to try and topple him, shove him over the rail to our left and take my chances. What did I have to lose?

All too soon we arrived at an unmarked door, and a rotting fear ate at my stomach. The guard wrenched it open and pointed into the dimly lit closet space. Inside was a single bed with a lone pillow, situated across from a mop bucket.

"You can sleep in here," he grunted, "Ten minutes only."

My limbs cried out for the mattress, as uncomfortable as this appeared. Would this guy seal the door and leave? Patience was not one of his qualities and he drew a strange weapon from his belt, aiming it at my chest. It looked enough like a gun for me to comply. Lord knows what kind of technology these people considered weapons.

I'd no sooner stepped towards the open closet than a shrill sound pierced the air. The tall guard shifted his view erratically, seeming to look for a sign of what was going on. The fear in my gut bubbled to adrenaline as I noticed he had completely forgotten I existed; I used the last of my strength to drive a shoulder into his bloated abdomen, knocking the wind out of him.

The gun clattered onto the floor.

With narrow arms, the guard linked one around the railing behind him and the other he tried to link around my waist. I pulled back, as far as his grip would allow, and made a second push, this time ousting him over the edge completely. The descending cry was paved over by the continuous screech of the alarm.

Scooping up the weapon, my screaming back promptly reminded me of this afternoon's waiting shift. I gritted my teeth and sprinted across the landing, hoping that I wouldn't tumble straight into the arms of one of the hosts.

Further down the deck I could just make out the outlines of Valdis's staff, panicking as they tried to reason with their awful customers. I smirked at the sight, slinking down the nearest staircase until I was on the ground floor. In the scarlet-lined thralls of what I imagined to be the Genesis's reception area, the two post-humans on the other side of the desk were locked in a heated argument.

The entrance doors sat opposite but wouldn't close. Then I saw why. Lodged between the door and wall was a body, its navy shirt and black waistcoat glistening with a sticky red. The door attempted to close, bounced off the face-down corpse, then retried.

"Oh shit, oh shit," I mumbled, breathing heavy. The weapon I had taken from the guard could well have been a pistol, its design complex and riddled with glowing buttons. Part of me wanted to risk it and try to open fire; if the body in the lobby was any indication of what a dash would result in, fighting might be the best option.

I panted, sweat teeming down my neck into the collar. The uniform made my skin itch as I stood idle in the stairway, fingers gripping the gun until my knuckles turned white.

Jogging down the last few steps, weapon raised, I saw the confused rage in the lobby staff's faces. Before they could pick up weapons of their own, a scolding hole erupted from both of their torsos. They slammed against the desk and moved no more. Standing on the stairs opposite me was another of their kind, a steaming rifle in its hands. His apparel matched my own.

"You're that girl, the new hire," he grimaced, weathered teeth showing.

"Who are you?"

"I'll tell you once we're out," the gunman puffed, "Maxim, a friend of mine, got into those bastards' defence network. Collar's are offline, if you want to run."

"To where?" I asked, staring at the pressing foliage lining the entranceway.

The guy scoffed, "Anywhere! Anywhere's better than here, no?"

At that moment, he was joined on the steps by another two like him, decked out in uniforms. They paused when they came into eyeline with me.

"Who's this, another runner?" one of them murmured.

Above our heads, the alarm harped on.

#

The terrain was rugged and covered with dense plant life. The world of two hundred and sixty-six million years ago was not what I had expected at all, and segments of my brain were struggling to accept it.

We'd run for as long as our legs could carry us, until the Genesis restaurant was a black speck on the horizon and the wailing siren had faded into the thick warmth of the dying day. Occasionally a creature of unknown origin would roar miles off. Other than that, we were accompanied only by our heavy breathing as we navigated the brush, led by the gunman from the lobby.

His name, as he muttered over his shoulder, was Vym and he appeared to have the lay of the land better than the others.

Maxim, his friend, had been the one to shut off the collar network supposedly; she brought up the rear. Keeping pace with me was another of their post-human kin, Allindra. Vym had to take this from her nametag as she couldn't speak a word.

After a lengthy spell on the move, Vym had guided us through a clearing into which the red prehistoric sky bled, clearing the wide leaves with both hands until a blackened doorway was revealed leading inside a sheer rock face. I was apprehensive about stepping into the cold dark, causing irritation to my new captor; Maxim walked with Allindra, and Vym shrugged at me, pacing off after them.

I took one last look at the outside world and crossed the threshold.

A further march for about a half-mile brought us to a wider section of the cave where others of Vym's kind lingered, whispering amongst themselves. It was here that we finally had a chance to sit and catch our breaths. Various cooked meats wrapped in leaves were brought to us as Vym mingled among the people. Questioning the meat for a second or two, I found that my stomach couldn't resist; I ravaged the lean flesh, leaving the bone in the tattered leaf on the rock by my side. I then spent minutes trying to suppress hiccups from eating so fast, much to the confusion of the folk in the cave.

Soon after, Vym returned and ushered me away from my seat, bringing me further into the heart of the cavern. Here the chalklike walls shrunk away, creating wide openings with alcoves where the post-humans huddled and slept. They watched me with curiosity as we strode by. Melting candles graced several of these recesses, the kind of table dressings I recognised from the dining area of the Genesis. The air was cooler in here, though brought about a damp smell with each step.

Halting in a corner, Vym nodded to a figure just out of view; he then turned to me, his eyes almost disapproving, and plodded out the way we had come.

Seconds later, the figure in the shadow made itself known. Its head stood taller than those I had seen up until now, wrapped in a piece of torn black cloth; it wore the same across its mouth and nose, partially, I imagined, due to the damp reek in the caverns. What was left of the clothes on its person were torn, including that of a cloak; this dragged along the floor of the cave, dipping into small pools as the being edged closer.

"You are a very strange creature, are you not?" its eyes narrowed. I didn't know how to respond, looking left and right for Vym. The reason I was brought to this darkened nook was not yet apparent, but I wagered it was about to be made so.

"Do you have a name?"

"Uh, Lucy. Lucy Cross."

"Odd, odd," the being shook its wrinkled dome, chattering to itself for a moment.

"And you are?"

It snapped out of its daze suddenly. "Kal Earon will suffice," and he motioned for me to sit by him on a flat outcrop. "Yes, very odd indeed. You are not like the regular kind the Genesis brings in, oh no."

A chill ran down my neck. "The regular kind?"

"Oh yes, the poor souls from the E.Zs! Didn't you pay attention during orientation?" spluttered Kal Earon, "Us, dear girl! Surely you have at least noticed you're different?"

"It occurred to me, " I said through gritted teeth, "I don't exactly belong here, as I tried to tell the management at the Genesis. But what do you know of that place? You seem to know *something*, at the very least."

Kal Earon shuffled in his seat. "It is unfortunate that I know of that horrid restaurant, a bastion of treachery at the beginning of time. Judging by your appearance, I'd wager you haven't seen the kind of atrocities that our people have; your hair, for one thing. It has been decades since I lost mine. And your skin! Not in any number of lifetimes could I have dreamt of having a complexion such as yours, for we are all born under the smoglines and see little of the sun, yes."

I scratched at my chin, ignoring the constant irritation of the uniform that I was still wearing, and watched as Kal Earon steadied his cranium against a slim palm, rising from his seat.

"Still, there will be time for discussion about our birthlands later. Or maybe not, and I hope not. There is much to plan, as we have been doing so for a long while. By now, even by primitive standards, you will have figured out that the Genesis is the heart of all temporal activity in this region. Labour is beamed in by the guild, the clientele beam in of their own accord; do you understand? How long have you been in their employ, Lucy?"

"Five hours, judging by the digital display I saw in the restaurant."

A look of surprise crossed Kal Earon's brow. "Impressive, very. It is doubtful you had much of an opportunity to explore the building. Few do. There are sentinels all over. Vym, who rescued you this evening, was previously one of them. He knows what truly goes on in the blackness below ground, where the darling eyes of the public are shielded from a reality so harsh, it would put them off their soup.

"Unfortunately, that foul sanctuary holds the only true escape to this prison on the edge of time, that being the means to send us home," the old man wandered the floor, lost in thought, "Or, indeed anywhere."

By this point, my own head was swimming. The shock of our
contraption back in Salt Lake City, housed in an unused gym hall in
the University of Utah, having actually generated a result and hurled
a pilot through the ages, was too much for my tired brain to
comprehend. Yet here I was, and not the only travellers at that! The
mental image of the dinosaur silhouette I had witnessed earlier
beyond the grounds of the Genesis flickered into my mind's eye, and
for the first time today, my thoughts were allowed to process.

Kal Earon, whether out of quiet curiosity or pity for a creature he
deemed underdeveloped, granted me a moment's peace and folded
his arms, leaning against the cavern walls. He shut his eyes and
would seem to be asleep for a good while, standing upright. After the
passing of several minutes, he approached again and gently shook
my shoulder.

"You are weary. It has most likely been a day filled with large
questions and little answers. I shall have one of our number make
you a bed for the night, and we can discuss more in the morning."

At the motion of Kal Earon's outstretched finger, a post-human
appeared and nodded for me to follow on. I glanced back only once,
seeing the old man lower his slender frame back onto his seat in the
alcove. His existence was raising many questions, however it was
nowhere near the point to be asking them.

I was shown to my own spot tucked to the side of the cavern wall,
not a far walk from Kal Earon's space. A thin blanket awaited me on
the ground.

Sleep came upon swiftly, despite the best efforts of the uniform and
collar gnawing at me as I lay. Eventually the shapes of the cavern's
people close by blurred into a mix of shades against a backdrop of
soft water droplets.

#

My segment of the cave was bathed in darkness when I woke. An
ever-weakening glow from candles could be seen further along the
winding passage, an orange glow throbbing against the gloom.

It took seconds for my eyes to grow accustomed to the surroundings,
but when they did, they picked out the shape of Vym perched
opposite where I lay, arms folded and back straight. His glower could
still be made out, even in the blackness of the nook.

"I have need of your help, new hire," he pointed a protracted finger towards the end of the passage, slinking off his perch and out of sight. He returned a second later with a bundle in his arms, dropping them on the ground and disappearing again. "Dress. And hurry." What the bundle held was an assortment of pelts and skins, of which animals I couldn't guess in my bleary state. They couldn't have been any itchier than the awful uniform that still clung to my body with perspiration, and I undressed, quickly wrapping up in some of the thicker brown furs. I left the discarded uniform in a pile next to the dreadfully uncomfortable shoes Valdis had picked for me, stumbling along the path to catch up with Vym.

He waited in a spot as the passage forked, waving me towards a narrow avenue that curved upwards and to the left, and led out onto a rocky shelf peering down the side of the mountain. A blanket of stars stretched out over the darkened sky, the moon high and waxing; a hundred feet below, bristles on conifers shook in the light breeze, the winds a welcome interruption in the thick humid night. Witnessing a land untouched by civilisation, untouched by the very ravages of onward-marching time was, for those brief moments, breathtaking.

 I crouched by Vym, resting on the balls of my feet as he leaned over the edge, searching the valley below. "A patrol passed through here tonight," he said, pulling himself back to a sitting position, "I haven't seen one in a long while, before tonight, I should say." He stared at me, expectantly. I shrugged. "Kal Earon believes you can help us, new hire. I'm not so sure. I also believe that the search team is on the hunt for you."

My blood ran cold at the thought of Vym turning me in, even rolling me down the jagged slopes.

"Why did you rescue me if you plan on turning me over to them?"

"That's not our intention. Maxim and I were pulling a raid, we do it every now and then. It's how we keep our numbers up, by freeing those the Genesis has had beamed in from our time. You just happened to start your shift on a very fortuitous day."

"So, what do you possibly need from me, if you can already break in and out of that place?"

Vym grunted, "Breaking in creates noise, raises the alarms. As you know, Maxim can interrupt their collar system no problem, but that's the least of the guards' worries when there's heavy gunfire erupting across the decks. I'd prefer we infiltrate, that way we can take our time and scope out the lower levels, places I've not seen the inside of. And with a technician—" he nodded at me, "—in our ranks, maybe crack the device that holds all the secrets: their temporal transporter. If our team can search, unhindered by alarms."

I rolled my head, shaking sleep from my mind.

"Kal Earon says you already know what goes on at the heart of the Genesis—"

"It is true that I used to be amongst their employ! The layout is fresh in my mind, though intricate details of their in-house time device and where it's kept are outside of my knowledge. I am aware of what goes on below the oak slats, out of the sun's reach, with regards to the labour after their shifts expire," said Vym, gravely mulling over the details, internally preparing them for me before my watchful gaze.

Multiple beams danced on the horizon. We lay low on our stomachs, slowing our breathing.

"Osric let slip that the restaurant has recently employed around eleven thousand staff," I whispered.

There was a pause. The lights in the distance drifted behind the foliage.

Sighing, Vym turned to me, eyes fixed to the ground. "Staff are worked until they expire, but they aren't sent back to the 39th century, as they'd have you believe."

"Do you know where they go, though?"

"Certainly. As soon as they drop, management carts them into the lower levels; they are given a bout of electroshock, and then laid in lead coffins and liquidised."

My wide eyes burned into the side of his bulbous head.

"Don't order the soup," he added.

I barely had the chance to ask a following question as I was silenced again. The beams in the valley were coming from lamps, a group of four figures rustling in the overgrown plants. As they neared the ridge where we hid, I saw their uniforms resembled something close to biohazard safety suits, baggy silver fabric with a dark plastic visor. Each one carried a weighty looking backpack, and long rifles upon which sat their lamps.

Leaning close, Vym cupped his hand. "The patrol I mentioned. We need their uniforms. With these, we can get four of my people into the Genesis."

A sickness brewed deep within me as my view darted between the lights in the darkness and the gunman crouched beside me. Wrapped in the pelts, Vym could have passed for a wild animal at that point, on the verge of pouncing.

Pulling one of the furs up and over his mouth and nose, he urged me to follow him down a faint path that curled down the cliff face, past the lip of the ridge. The patrol kept their sights low to the ground, thankfully, and the beams did not trouble us. We gradually worked our way down, edging to the jungle floor down the narrowest of pathways. My foot then clipped a cleft of gravel over the side, scattering stones over the waiting plantlife and conjuring a sound like artificial rain on their descent. I clapped a hand over my mouth, gasping.

Vym shot an angered look back.

Surprisingly, the four did not seem to notice. Instead, they appeared to be getting fed up with searching the area and were preparing to move on.

Dropping the last few feet to the floor, I trailed after Vym as we crawled into the dense green world. The beams shifted focus, searching the trees opposite, and swaying as if affected by the breeze. All four silver-clad patrolmen had their backs to us, unaware of the impending danger from the enraged post-human approaching like a snake in the grass.

His movements were fluid, as if he had been hunting his entire life. It was difficult to image Vym growing up in the 3800s, as it had been drip-fed to me, it sounded like they lived a mostly urbanised lifestyle within the ruins of the E.Zs. Yet his skill with his bare hands alone was astounding; shortly after, he would explain that he did not want to sully the patrol uniforms with blood by using a weapon, as that would render the disguise next to useless on arrival. He also clearly did not want my help or any kind of intervention on my part, opting to subdue his prey one by one and at a pace that suited him, and him alone.

As the fourth neck was snapped and the valley was deemed safe again, Vym extended his back and waved to me over the waist-high leaves.

"It is done," he panted, "These garments will allow us entry."

"These are too large for me," I tapped at one of the bodies buried in the vegetation, the realisation that they were freshly dead not quite sitting with me yet.

"That is true, they will not fit a primitive of your size. Teams such as these are only deployed when the collars fail. Management prefers the fabric of time outwith their walls be left undisturbed," said Vym, crouching and slowly rotating the body. Under the glow of the moon, he fished around in the backpack, his spindly fingers digging into each of the pouches. He unclipped the top segment, unrolling a black plastic sheath the length of the patrolman's corpse.

"This," he motioned, "is how you will get back into the Genesis."

#

Thump.

Thump.

Beads of sweat collected on my forehead and the back of my neck, my suspended body crashing against the insides of the plastic cocoon.

Thump.

I wrestled my hand through the minute opening above, pushing the zip away and stretching the opening. The night air was warm still, offering little refreshment.

"Quiet, we're nearing the restaurant," came Vym's gruff voice, dampened by the plastic. "You'll get the signal when we're in."

The trip lasted longer than I had anticipated, my breathing becoming more laboured with each lurch of the bag. At the front and back of the container were two of Vym's people, dressed in the disguise of the patrol group; Vym himself strode alongside, though I could not figure out which side he was on with his voice muffled as it was. Another was meant to be bringing up the rear.

His mood had remained sour during the planning phase. Their cover story was to be that they had caught and killed a member of Kal Earon's tribe in the wild, bagged them up and brought them in for liquidation. The term, coupled with the intense heat in the body bag, made me want to vomit.

Thump.

Voices came and went, all suppressed to my ears. Some were raised, most were calm.

A steady descent followed, part of me worrying that I would slide out the bottom and crash out onto the floor in the middle of a crowded corridor. Then it really would be game over.

Thump. Thump.

Soon the unforgiving hard touch of the floor nestled into my back, and the upper corners of the plastic sheath deflated around me like a circus tent being taken down at the end of a show. As I attempted to wriggle free of the bondage, a low voice grumbled close to me.

"Don't move, lie still, say nothing."

I paused, pushing my body flat against the floor. The pistol I had taken from my jailor before the escape now pressed into my ribs, and it took a moment of shuffling to find a position that didn't cause further agony.

"We'll be back for you in twenty minutes," said the voice that sounded like Vym's. "Keep breathing," he chuckled as the four pairs of boots stomped off, their echoing footfalls fading gradually.

How long I lay there, I had no idea. My thoughts kept flitting back to 2076, to my team that were undoubtedly hovering around our original time device in that gym hall in Utah; imagining their panicked expressions was a bittersweet comfort, and I wished I could reappear in a puff of smoke and hear their mingling voices. I longed to just know that everything was alright, or at least would be.

Although I had no watch, I felt that twenty minutes had come and gone and had not brought Vym and his friends back. Peeping through the slot in the zip, I could make out only the yellow glow of the ceiling lights and the smooth grey flooring that they cast their rays on.

"And here they are!"

Every muscle tensed at once. The voice was close, familiar too. Were they standing over me?

"Let's have a look at you, shall we?"

Valdis!

I gripped the pistol tight, perspiration squeezing from a numbed palm. Sensory deprivation caused me to panic, imagining the spidery hands latching around the zip and peeling it back.

With one great flick of her wrist, the zip whirred down. I rolled onto my back, pistol drawn in the shocked face of the Genesis restaurant's supervisor. She picked at her cravat, panting as I crawled out of my cocoon. The room was a lot smaller than I initially thought; cabinets covered most of the walls, and, more concerningly, a stack of neatly folded black body bags, similar to my own, sat in one corner.

I nudged the door shut, pistol trained on Valdis. She gathered her next line carefully, recovering from a genuine shock to her withered heart.

"Well, Lucy, I never expected to see you again. Certainly not alive, at any rate."

It was obvious she was judging the animal pelts that were wrapped around my skin, a mocking grin stripping my soul bare. I shook this off, taking a step towards her, pistol aimed at her swelled cranium. "I suspect that this little game has been perpetrated by Kal Earon? Would I be correct?" Valdis regained some of her lost composure, rubbing at her sunken chin. "Yes, the madman in the jungle—"
"I'm surprised you know him," I muttered, heart crashing in my chest.
"Sadly, we do know of him. He did work here, for a spell."
"One of your management? Or one of the 'countless thousands of lucky individuals' the Genesis plucked from the future?"
Valdis snickered, her top lip protruding.
"He was management, Lucy. Back then, you'd have found him a much fouler individual than I, I can tell you. Kal loathed labour beamed in from the guild. He'd remark that their minds weren't up for the challenge of providing six-star dining service after years of nuclear fallout and bone idleness. Did I agree with everything he ever came out with? No—"
And she inched closed to the barrel of the pistol. I slid a foot back, preparing for Valdis to attempt to rush me.
"—Nonetheless, he was Genesis, through and through. He just doesn't agree with management *these days*, or when it suits him, it seems! Launches his silly attacks with Vym and the other squatters because the company won't send them back."
"No? And why won't they? Might save you folk a lot of hassle."
"Their contracts have been terminated; they have left the business. Kal and Vym abandoned their posts, left without notice! I don't know what time *you're* from, Lucy, but that is not business etiquette here!"
"2076…" I blurted out.
"Excuse me, dear?"
"I'm from 2076!" I pulsed towards the post-human, watching her shrivel into a shaking heap as the gun neared her chest. My nerves were burning, every inch of me alight with fury and exhaustion. "I have told you numerous goddamn times: I'm from 2076! I wasn't sent by the Employment Guild, and I'm glad of it!"
"Okay, okay—"

"Kal Earon already told me you had a time device here, so I have to thank you for confirming that," I nearly smirked at Valdis's ghostly pale face. I pulled the weapon away from her; as awful of a person as she was, seeing her tremble because of me was a fresh kind of sickness that I wanted to shake off immediately. "Now, I'm going to ask you politely, and I hope that you'll see reason. Can you please send me home?"

Valdis's thin lips crinkled into a fresh smile, the first wholesome expression she had made since we'd met.

"I- I can," and she wiggled her fingers around her neck, "I can also get that off for you." And she pointed at the collar still fixed around my throat; putting up with it had become second nature now.

Pistol raised, I allowed Valdis to approach. Her spiced perfume lingered in the air as she worked; and work fast she did. The black band separated and fell away into her hand, and she gingerly slunk back into the corner of the room. I contemplated offering my thanks, figuring I should save that until after she had done what I initially asked. Instead, I motioned towards the door with the pistol, Valdis shimmying along the back wall on command, knowing where she had to take us.

"You know, you're much more civilised than I gave you credit for," spoke Valdis over her shoulder, the gun now resting in her lower back as she reached for the door. "You aren't one of Vym's crew at all. Certainly not of the same ilk as Kal Earon."

I ignored her as we entered the hallway, the passage too cramped for two. She trudged onwards, on the lookout for other members of staff; on the rare instance when someone was in the vicinity, Valdis gave me a signal and I held back, keeping her hunched spine within arm's reach. Moving down another flight of stairs, the building's layout appeared to alter in the lower floors. Corridors were curved, as if encircling some inner chamber, and I began to get the feeling that we were drawing closer to the epicentre of the Genesis.

Relief washed over me on seeing an empty reception desk in these lower levels as cover was lacking, especially with there being no corners to duck behind. Seeing as we were alone again, Valdis resumed her speech.

"As I was previously saying, Lucy, I understand you to be far above the intellect of those savages with which you ran. Vym is clever in his own right, but a known troublemaker with no respect for the rules. You understand the rules, and you played by them for a strong five hours, though you are clearly displaced in time. I appreciate that, as does the company," she reduced her volume at the sound of voices rising from an adjacent corridor. We increased our step.

"What's your point?" I whispered, ducking between Valdis and the wall.

"Dear girl, my point, as you so bluntly put it, is that you are not *them*, as much as they are not you. Why, what was Vym's plan? To leave you in a corpse carrier on the floor for anyone to find?"

I exhaled, shivering slightly.

"They wouldn't tell you the plan, would they?" she grinned, her pointed tongue running along the row of discoloured teeth. "Good gracious, Lucy! And these are the people you're in league with!"

I butted the barrel into her lower back, "Keep your goddamn voice down."

We moved twenty paces down the hall, Valdis's flat shoes clopping loudly on the wooden floors. Stopping at a room on the bend, she produced a blue keycard made of a gleaming plastic and slid it into a reader slot on the wall; the metallic door slid apart, and we continued inside.

"I see no reason for you to keep that thing drawn on me after I have already agreed to help you," Valdis said over her shoulder. "I am assisting you of my own desire to right my previous mistake, not out of fear for my own skin." She reached over to a panel on her right and yanked the lever that hung from it. White spotlights on the ceiling burst into life; I shielded my eyes for a second. "All I would kindly ask is a favour in return, before you go hopping off in our machine." And Valdis waved at the chair in the centre of the room, installed on a dais and surrounded by a ring of chest-high racks.

I couldn't help but stare in wonder at the device. It had a more basic aesthetic to it than I had imagined theirs would, expecting a velvet-coated seat and gold handrails as opposed to a lightly padded chair of steel construction with no frills. Perhaps due to it being so far-removed from the public that this utility was treated as such: no pomp necessary.

Valdis gauged the look on my face and linked her hands, tapping the tips together.

"Here you have it, as promised. Your window to the future," she gestured, like a salesman entering the final stages of a pitch, "Can I ask but one favour in return, now?"

"If you must," I sighed.

"Excellent. You are, without a doubt, eager to depart. We, on the other hand, are eager to keep our activities within the boundaries of the restaurant, as I believe you recall."

I nodded, remembering Osric's lecture from yesterday.

"The runaways you encountered are thus in breach of several temporal laws, even just by living out in the wild," Valdis looked me up and down, her reddened fish-like eyes glazing over on further inspection of the furs wrapped around my hips and breasts. "Why, the clothes they have gathered from the hides of the creatures of the Mesozoic are in violation of so many laws, it makes my head spin! Aside from that matter, I would much prefer you inform the company of wherever their… den, is, if you can call it that. Where do they do their scheming?"

Clicking a button on the side of the touchpad in her blazer pocket, Valdis held it out to me. On the dark orange screen there glowed a rugged outline snaking away from a central square marked 'Gen'. I began to identify sections of this map, remembering the paths used to escape the restaurant, and the alcove in the rock face shown to us by Vym. I looked at Valdis, her short-lived wholesome smile mutating into something much more sinister.

Apprehensive, I raised my hand to the glow of the screen.

"What do you intend to do?"

"Welcome them back, of course!" Valdis's lips turned black as she scrunched them together, "Though I understand they will undoubtedly view this as an act of hostility, management would much rather see them brought inside the complex rather than risking the human race's timeline by having them dwelling in the wilds, interacting with the flora and fauna."

"Small acts can create large ripples," I murmured, a line told to me by Eddie Warwick, another tech from our team. My heart ached thinking of them, and of dreaming of Salt Lake City itself. The line landed with Valdis, as she nodded her wobbling head in agreement.

"You speak the truth, Lucy. Who knows what damage will have been caused by their reckless endeavours, centuries from now?"

A shudder passed down my spine. This might be the only opportunity I get to escape back to my own time. For all I knew, Vym and his team had been captured and processed already.

I pointed to the location of the cave on the map, a sinking feeling coming over me.

#

A torrent of clicking came from the keyboard as Valdis configured the machine, claiming it hadn't been used in many weeks. I was quick to remind her that I wouldn't hesitate to shoot her down if she tried to alert the staff; so far, she had kept her word.

"I merely passed the coordinates you gave me on to Roth," she hissed from the console, "You can lower that weapon, Lucy. There are no patrols waiting to storm this room, if that's what you're worried about."

I watched over her shoulder at the screens of symbols scrolling upwards, grateful to myself for not killing her at first sight. I didn't know why Vym assumed I would be able to tinker with this contraption any better than he could. The language on display was completely alien.

After a period, a series of thuds ruptured from outside the door. Shouts followed, then sounds of an ensuing scuffle. On the edge of her seat, Valdis was poised to leap up and investigate, until I reminded her that it would be a bad idea. The minutes wore on, time crawling at a snail's pace until she gave me the all-clear.

"You are safe to enter, Lucy," Valdis sighed, the most deflated I had seen her, "If you could leave the pelts, the company would be eternally grateful."

Resigned, I stripped myself of the warm furs and clambered into the steel seat on the dais, the platform sharply cold on my bare feet. Valdis obediently assisted, swinging the heavy clamps across my ankles and wrists. She slipped the pistol from my grasp and set it down on the table next to the pelts; my hand suddenly felt naked without it. I started to wonder just where on Earth the time device would send me, where I would end up after passing through a jump. The shouting in the hall intensified.

Valdis had no sooner returned to her own seat than the console began emitting a bleeping sound. Scooping up a headset from the desk, she answered a call, to which I could only hear from her side. It was news that pleased her, at any rate, and that meant a more positive outcome for me.

"Well, you have come through for us, Lucy," her face creased with delight, "Roth followed your coordinates, and his team has not long since returned."

"They didn't kill any of them, did they?" I asked, irritated at how childlike I sounded.

"There were some casualties. Kal Earon would not go quietly, but we have the majority of his followers in custody," Valdis scratched at the cracked skin under her hairpiece, "And we have you to thank for fixing our little time traveller problem."

"And Vym?"

"He will be furious, but I fear his end is closer than he realises. I will leave it to Roth and his people to sniff them out. They can't have gone far."

She clacked on the keyboard again and the machinery around me whirred and groaned. Stepping awkwardly onto the platform beside me, Valdis adjusted a steel band from the headrest of my seat, pressing it onto my sweat-stained brow.

The din in the hallway died down until it was buried beneath the humming of the fans in the racks. It occurred to me that the commotion may have been the rest of Vym's people being dragged into custody by their new jailors. Their screaming voices stabbed through the white noise at regular intervals, a harrowing ghostly wail reminding me of what Vym had told me up on the ridge.

My eyes widened as the solitary door to the chamber slid open and in waddled another post-human, dressed sharply in a black suit one size too small for him. He was pushing a cart towards us.

As he neared, I understood what it was. A casket made of solid lead. Valdis gave me an almost apologetic look as she saw the fear in me, saw me hysterically trying to shift my limbs under the weight of the clamps.

"This will take about fifteen minutes," she mused, though whether she was talking to me or just to the stale chamber air, I would never know.

Flitting her sunken eyes, Valdis strolled towards the door, waving back just the once.

I shouted myself hoarse, the crackle of electrodes gathering around me like a storm.

"The primitive being discharged, is that right?" asked the casket-bearer.

"Oh yes," mumbled Valdis, adjusting her bouffant as it lurched to one side, "Her shift at the Genesis is complete. Save the hair from this one, if you can."

I could just make out her winking at me before she strutted out, the heavy door sliding closed in her wake.

S.R Malone is a writer living just outside Edinburgh, Scotland. He has been published in Synthetic Reality Magazine, 365 Tomorrows, AntipodeanSF, and Spillwords. When he is not writing or reading, he likes to play video games and spend time with his family and their dog, going for long walks. Get in touch at srmaloneauthor.com

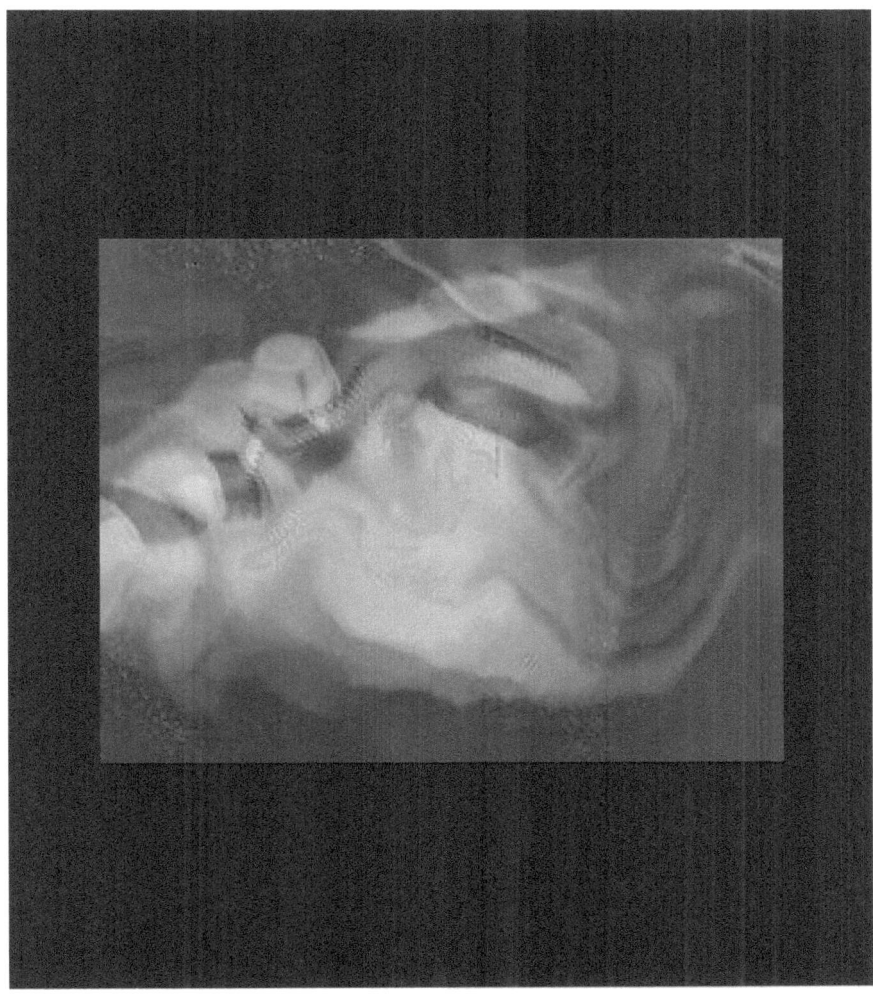

Other Anthologies available from
Neon Sunrise Publishing:

A LIGHT THAT
NEVER GOES OUT

A Neon Sunrise Anthology

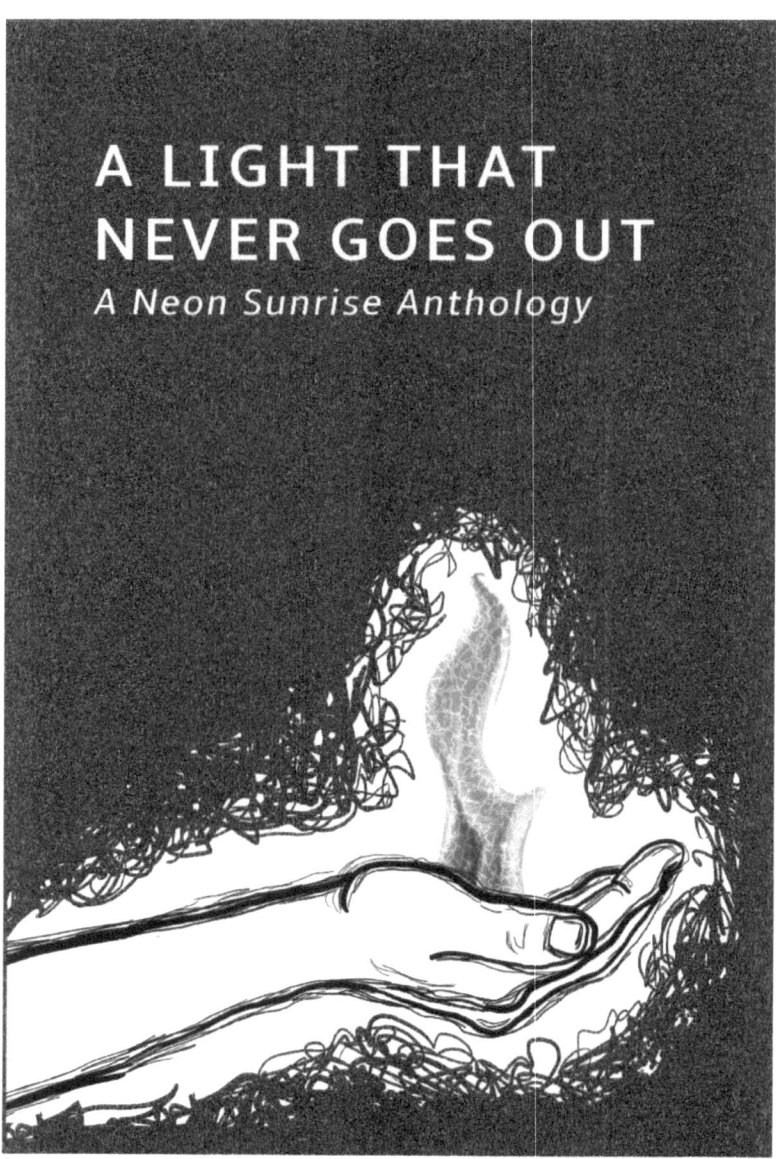

A NEON SUNRISE ANTHOLOGY

Neon Sunrise Publishing is focused on helping independent creators realize their dreams of seeing their books in print. We're driven by a DIY spirit and a desire to provide options and resources to help developing talent succeed in sharing their voice with the world.

To keep up with all of our latest news and releases, be sure to join our mailing list and connect with us online!

Email:	**neonsunrisepub@gmail.com**
Facebook:	**facebook.com/neonsunrisepub**
Instagram:	**@neonsunrisepub**
Twitter:	**@neonsunrisepub**
Website:	**www.neonsunrisepublishing.com**